The Pure
And The Hated

WildBluePress.com

For Page

The Pure
And The Hated

1.

Marigold and Joyce lived in the house by the red barn that passing tourists used to photograph. They came to that part of Vermont for the skiing. They'd hit the slopes, fill the restaurants, and leave with their memories. I envy them now. I wish I could exchange my memories for those of another man. I have no vacations left inside me.

The drive I took from Stowe to visit my nieces once made my heart ache with its beauty, but in the end that gentle road leading into the mountains felt like a scar. I used to help Marigold and Joyce with their reading when they were little. My sister, Holly, did so much for them. Their father, Dwight Fisher, had run off years ago, no one knew where, leaving her alone. That was before they were born. He returned off and on; he had a knack for doing that. He spent a few years with my sister, watched her get pregnant and neglected her. Then he vanished for good one summer's day, leaving her to bring her daughters up on her own. She never spoke of him, but reverted to the family name of Butler.

Having lost my own son, Felton, to a hunting accident, I came to feel Marigold and Joyce were like two daughters to me. My wife, Mary, never recovered from Felton's death. She said the loss of a child ended something inside her. Her maternal care seemed to wither. The kitchen was full of dead flowers for many months after his loss. She liked Marigold and Joyce but rarely visited them. And it seemed to me that

I was pouring all my paternal instincts into the two girls, wanting to protect them when I had been unable to save my own son's life. The fool is protected by his folly. I never envisaged the cruelty that life held in its card-dealing hands. I never saw what was to come. Perhaps that is why I became the man I am, a barely recognisable sum of memories that have altered my image and bruised my heart. I wish I could erase them, but they feed on me. The deepest bruise of all dwells like a swollen rose inside me, reminding me of that time with its thorns, that wounding time that violated us all.

Everything changed in those years, apart from the landscape. Its beauty in the fall still stops my breath; the green mountains of Vermont and shades of shifting colour overwhelm me. The vistas of clear brooks and streams. The hills flowing into mountains tell me that the earth is wiser than us.

My sister and nieces lived outside Stowe, beneath Mount Mansfield that always seemed to be sleeping, waiting for snow. I sometimes think it watched the events as they unfolded. The countryside there has a purity to it that is endlessly consoling. And to a certain kind of man that purity may aggravate his own sense of corruption, engendering thoughts of defilement.

The tourists came and went, brought money and took away stories and snapshots. They faded like invisible ink. But there was one man who passed through and left something ineradicable behind in those violated years. He passed through all right. He did so like a scythe that cut all certainty from my life and left me with thoughts that were alien to my soul. Temple Jones. There was no way of knowing him or predicting what he would do.

I remember something Mary said to me about him, 'Shepherd Butler, sometimes you just can't know a man;

some men keep things too well hidden.'

And what Temple Jones did to Mary was nothing compared to what he went on to do. He stole my understanding of the world and handed me back a reality that lacks all consolation. I crave the solace of purity and find only hatred. And I know that innocence is an affront to some men.

Even the well outside the window seems corrupted by the memory of him sitting there, his face reflected in the window pane. But I have other memories. I try to reach back to a time when I didn't know him and the world seemed good. I remember the sandstone well many years ago one sunlit morning in the early years of my marriage. It glowed like honeycomb and beneath me Mary's face was full of a fertile joy I have never known another woman to have. She tasted of mountain streams as I kissed her mouth, and I lived in a world of certainty as she took me inside her on the wet grass.

I am sure that was the day Felton was conceived, there beneath the well in the quiet privacy of our Vermont garden. My fingers smelt of wild columbine and sweetgrass, and Mary was mine, as was the future in all its broken knowledge. My wife had the purest skin, there was not a scar on her body, and as I touched her I was conscious my hands had been rooting in the soil, as if I was unfit for her body and all it would allow. But she yielded to me and gave me things I would never have dared ask from her. There was no restraint or inhibition in her touch, which gave permission to my desire. The marks she carries now can't be seen. Her sapphire blue eyes that once would search my face have faded, and while I inhabit the same house as her I have to reach into the past to feel her reality.

Her alabaster skin, her mouth, her erotic lips parted as I entered her on the pure earth, her full breasts and strong thighs, exist in a moment that has been removed from me, as she has been stolen from herself. I feel the ache of an amputated limb and want to dwell inside her again, but robbers have invaded our home and carried us away.

I am unmanned by events beyond my control and seek the feminine to prove myself again. I have become the castrated father of the tribe, my children are butchered, my possessions looted. That is the purpose that hatred serves. But I will not yield to that poisoned Bible. There was a time before corruption. I seek to separate the past from the wounds he inflicted. His deeds invaded us like a virus, replicating their own hatred inside us, taking away the things we once believed in. And while I can still see myself making love to Mary that day, I can also smell the fresh grass and see the columbine's spurs and feel the ones that Temple Jones wore cutting into my sides, as if he was on my back without my knowing, all along, even then.

2.

Late fall. Vermont a swathe of colour, scarlet and gold shimmering in the hills, banks of red leaves bleeding at the edges. Unearthly light. I was standing in the kitchen with Mary, finishing a cup of coffee and about to leave to visit Holly and the girls. Mary was dressed in a white blouse buttoned to the top. It complimented the beauty of her slender neck with its well-defined muscles. I see myself kiss the vein that runs across it. I feel it throb against my lips when we make love.

'Fall used to be my favourite season, Shepherd,' she said. 'But now all it does is remind me of Felton's death.'

'Do you want to come with me today?'

'I'm best on my own.'

'They'd love to see you.'

'Would they?'

I looked into her sky blue eyes, but they were wandering away from me. She gazed into the distance, at the mountains. Her hazelnut hair shone with light. I wanted to touch it.

'He knew you were proud of him,' I said.

'Did I tell him enough? Did I hold back my love in the name of duty as a parent?'

'You've never held anything back.'

'The beauty outside my window is too hard to bear. I don't want to see how unchanged it all is, how it keeps to its own aesthetic.'

I didn't understand what she meant, but I was to find out. My words fell like fake money from my mouth.

'Mary, I wanted the world to stop when he was shot. I felt as though tomorrow was a lie. We train ourselves to think of the future of our offspring, most of what we do as parents is a way of investing in that, and we never expect them to be taken from us. Part of the future goes with them. I know you didn't like him to hunt, but nothing would have persuaded him it was wrong.'

'I see them bringing back the deer on their cars, and it all seems so trivial to me now, my principles about killing animals. I wonder whether it was something else I was feeling when I tried to stop him from doing it, as if behind my views lay an unease, a sense he might come to harm out there.'

'You had the same principles at college.'

'Go on your own, Shepherd, send them my love. I'm not good company. I'm locked inside that fall two years ago. Do you remember us walking up Mount Mansfield, your hand in mine and Felton walking before us? I look at myself now, and I'm someone else.'

That ravaged morning I wanted to make love to my wife. As I kissed her good-bye I felt her desolation. Felton's death was lodged like a fish hook inside us.

I drove to Holly's, out of Stowe and its neat line of houses, and up the mountain road into the dying leaves and my shallow dreams of family life. As I pulled up I glanced at my face in the rearview mirror. I thought I could see someone else lurking behind my eyes, laughing at me. I stepped out of my pickup into the cold and felt like someone had punched a block of ice into my lungs.

Holly saw me walking up and opened the door.

'I got some fresh coffee on,' she said.

'Then I better help you drink it.'

Her house smelled of freshly baked bread. Holly kept it immaculate. It instilled a sense of ambiguity in me. It was a home, something I once knew, and inasmuch as that comforted me, it also tormented me with my loss.

Marigold and Joyce were sitting in the living room. They got up when they saw me walk in.

Marigold offered me her cheek.

'Hello, Uncle Shepherd.'

'We going out today?' Joyce said, standing on tiptoe so I could reach hers.

'If you want to.'

'Mom wants to go shopping,' Marigold said.

'Well let's talk to her about it. Now where's this coffee?'

Holly poured me a cup as my nieces chattered to each other. Marigold was nineteen and Joyce seventeen, and they both had a freshness to their looks that made them seem out of place it the modern world. They'd inherited Holly's beauty, but Marigold had darker eyes than her mother and Joyce a rosiness to her complexion that made me think of apples at harvest time. My sister was a dark blonde with deep brown eyes. Both Marigold and Joyce resembled her, having her small and delicate nose. But Marigold had black hair, while Joyce was a brunette with blue eyes she'd inherited from her father, who was a handsome man. I'd always suspected that Dwight Fisher had run off with another woman. Rumours had circulated about his behaviour when he disappeared, and I tried to keep them from my sister's ears. I'm not sure how much she heard, but I think gossip is harmful.

My own resemblance to Holly was a comfort to me. I looked at her and thought how we had the same colour eyes. Since Felton's death I felt as though I'd lost my family. Mary's isolation added to that. My grief was briefly lifted on those visits to Holly. But I wasn't the man I used to be, and I felt like an outsider. The tragedy had turned me grey, and I'd often look at my face in the bathroom mirror on rising as if I was staring at a stranger and think my beard was the colour of ash. I seemed without colour, grizzled, as if some part of me had been erased. And I took solace in the hues of the countryside and in my nieces.

For a while at times with the death of my son I felt my world had turned to ash. I took warmth from my nieces and stepped outside the black and white film I lived in at home when I visited them. They allowed me to think of the future.

As I looked at them I thought how these young women would have families and children in a few years, and I felt my loss tug at my heart. I dislodged the pain with a preoccupation I'd developed in the past year. I'd begun to feel responsible for my nieces, and I wondered how they would be employed when they were older.

I owned a hardware store in Stowe, and although I worked fewer hours in those days, and let my staff make decisions a few years ago I wouldn't have felt comfortable delegating, I worked as much as my grief would allow. Marigold had got good grades at school and was studying biology at the University of Vermont. She wanted to become a vet. Joyce had done less well and was looking for work. I'd just lost a member of staff at the shop, and I thought about offering Joyce the vacancy.

'How's the job search going?' I said.

Holly grinned.

'You mean you haven't told him, Joyce?' she said.

'Mom.'

'She's got a job.'

'Working in the Peoples' Bank, thanks to my math grades,' Joyce said. 'At least I was good at one subject at school.

'That's not true, Jo, you were good at science,' Marigold said.

'Not as good as you.'

'Will you two stop it?' Holly said. 'I'm just delighted she's got work, and at a bank, don't you think, Shepherd?'

'That's great news, Joyce.'

That afternoon we went into Stowe, and I helped Holly shop at Shaw's. We bought fresh lobster and chicken, and she stocked up on cans of vegetables and pasta.

'My car will be out of the shop in two days,' she said as we loaded my pickup with the bags.

'In the meantime if you need me to run you anywhere.'

'Thanks, Shepherd. How about coming back and sharing some of the chicken with us?'

'Sounds too good to resist.'

Back at her house, Holly chopped the chicken up and cooked it in a tomato sauce as I talked to the girls. We had it steaming hot with winter squash. As I ate I felt redundant as an uncle in a way I couldn't define.

I left after lunch and stopped on my way home to walk in Mount Mansfield State Forest. My visit had left me feeling unsettled, and I wanted to find out why. I began to wonder whether I secretly resented Holly the children she still had. And I thought of Mary alone, at home. I walked without looking where I was going. The woods felt like a womb.

As I entered a clearing I saw a man in threadbare clothes sitting on a log. He looked like some forest dweller who lives on berries and plants and is wild.

I'd wandered quite far in before I spotted him and was overcome by a sense of intrusion. He seemed to be hiding. Beside him was a fire and the burnt out remains of food. I could smell recently cooked meat.

I was about to turn away to leave him to his solitude when he raised a hand in greeting. I walked towards him.

There was a moment before I spoke when I felt this young man had some wisdom that I sought, as if my trip into the forest had a purpose beyond my desire to dispel my troubled thoughts. He had unkempt hair and fair features, a handsome face beneath the beard, but there was something about his looks that echoed in me in a sympathetic way and made me feel my walk into the forest had found its purpose in another human being.

'I didn't mean to intrude on you,' I said.

He stood up, wiped his hand on his faded corduroys, and extended it warmly.

'If I had any turkey left I'd offer you some. I'm not a bad cook.'

'Wild turkey?'

He smiled. It was a warm smile that lacked all guile, and I instantly warmed to him.

'I didn't buy it from a store.'

'Are you living out here?'

'I am, Sir.'

He said it with pride, pulling his shoulders back as he did.

I looked beyond him to the reds and golds in the trees.

'It will be hard for you in a few weeks; winter's coming on.'

'I'll make do; I've lived outside in seven feet of snow before. No need to worry about me.'

'Food will be scarce.'

'I know where to find it, and as I say, I cook well, that's what I was trained to do.'

'You're a chef?'

'I am, Sir. I worked in some of the finest restaurants in New England, worked out on Cape Cod. I make the best sauces, and now I rustle up some meat and plants. Say, why don't you come back and visit me, and I'll let you sample what I'm talking about? Nothing better than fresh food caught outdoors.'

'I can't argue with that.'

I recalled the many barbecues I'd made and the fresh game Mary and I used to take on our walks with Felton.

'I know these woods well. I walk here often,' I said. 'You must feel solitary.'

'I like to keep my own company after what happened to me.'

I hesitated before I asked the next question, cautious of intruding on his privacy, feeling as though I'd already strayed into his home, but there was something deeply familiar about him, and he aroused an intense curiosity in me.

'What did happen to you?' I said.

'It's a long story.'

'I have time.'

He looked into the distance.

'I fell in love with a woman,' he said, 'the most beautiful woman I've ever seen. I was working towards owning my own restaurant and borrowed money heavily for our future. We were going to get married. Anna Belle was her name. We were a few months away from getting hitched when she was shot dead by an obsessed man.'

'My God.'

'It snapped me in two. I couldn't work, my debts mounted, and I lost my job and house. I confess I wanted to kill him. But my daddy was a preacher. The Bible is my only possession apart from my pans and what you see me wearing. I decided to live apart from human society. The killer walked free; he wasn't punished. To deal with my sense of injustice I knew I had to get away. I journeyed into the wilderness seeking forgiveness.'

'Forgiveness?'

'I want to forgive him to free myself of the burden he's laid on my soul. By depriving myself of the luxuries of life, the things I once enjoyed, I'm seeking to understand him and be free of the pain in my heart. You could say I'm here in search of Christ. The desire for revenge is a terrible thing. It will eat you alive. I'll never forget what he did and my struggle with it has made me aware of my own impurity.'

'You're a remarkable man. Anyone would want revenge in such circumstances, but don't you think you're punishing yourself?'

'I don't see living outdoors as punishment. There are people living in conditions far worse than mine.'

'I understand what grief can do. I share some of your pain; I lost a son to a hunting accident.'

'That's a terrible thing, a truly terrible thing, for a parent to lose their child.'

'We live our lives with assumptions.'

There were tears in his eyes, and I noticed how deeply

green they were, like polished jade in a clear pool of water.

'I'm ashamed,' he said.

'Of what?'

'Myself, standing here talking of my troubles when you have worse. It shows me how far I am from Christ.'

I laid a hand on his shoulder, feeling mainly bone.

'I think you're closer than you realise.'

'I sometimes wonder if Christ is as hard to get to know as a man. There are depths to some men we can never fathom.'

'I don't think you ought to live out here with winter coming on.'

'I can survive the cold.'

As I stood there I saw Felton's body when we found him lying in a carpet of leaves. Their beauty was an insult to the injury that embedded itself in my soul that day.

'Hunters come through here; I wouldn't want to see you injured,' I said.

'I don't know much about hunting, I disapprove of guns. But I don't believe the shooting season's started yet.'

'It's a few weeks off.'

'I don't mean to pass judgement on hunting, but after what happened to Anna Belle …'

'I understand.'

'A gun's too easy for a man to use. That killer walked right into our house and shot Anna Belle dead, riddled her body with bullets. Now, he could have been carrying a knife, but you might say that would give her more chance to get away. We live in a great country consumed by gun culture.'

'My wife would agree with you.'

'Because your boy was shot?'

'Mary was always opposed to guns. But he wasn't shot.'

'I thought you said he was hunting.'

'He was. Bow and arrow deer season, right about now. He used the bow because of his mother's feelings about guns; he was a good shot. It was an arrow that killed him. It went right through his neck. Felton bled to death alone.'

'What happened to the man responsible?'

'We never found out who he was. Although the papers were full of the story, no one came forward. He must have been too scared to face up to what he did. So you see we share a loss and an injustice.'

'We do.'

'Well, I better be going back; dusk's coming. It was good talking to you.'

'Likewise, Sir.'

'I don't even know your name.'

'Maxwell Heed.'

'Shepherd Butler.'

I shook his hand again.

I walked into the forest, glancing back once to see him reading his Bible, then I found the road and drove back to Mary. And all the way there I thought of Felton and what it was I had wandered into the forest to find. And I realised my paternal instincts were seeking an outlet. I thought about Maxwell out there, in the dark. I thought about him when I saw the fire crackling in our kitchen and Mary standing by the cooker making supper. She turned to me and I kissed her. And I wondered if she would understand and if solitude gave anyone the things they needed.

3.

I told her about him. I told her how I'd found him there and of the things he said.

Mary ate while I described him and the way he was living. She said nothing, and I began to feel as though my words were irritating her. I wondered what we had left, two parents with a shared and irrevocable loss. When I mentioned his views on guns she looked up and laid her knife and fork down on her plate. She looked at me for some time as I carried on, and I could tell she felt some affinity, as I did, for Maxwell. I told her my concerns for him when the rifle deer season began.

She looked past me at the picture that sat on a table against the wall. It showed Felton in the forest and was taken some weeks before he died. Then she stood up and walked to the window. She stood there for some time staring out at the night.

'What do you want to do, Shepherd?' she said. 'It seems this young man has some relevance beyond that of a passing stranger for you.'

'He's out there with a tragedy inside him. He shares our loss. I wonder if he will survive.'

'What is it you want to give to him? Shelter?'

'Possibly.'

'Or is it more? Is it you trying to fill the hole, the way

you do with Marigold and Joyce?'

'Perhaps. Is that so wrong?'

'We grieve in different ways.'

'Mary, is isolation enough for you?'

'I don't call it isolation.'

'You were a great mother, why let that part of you wither and die?'

'I feel sterile; you must feel it when you make love to me.'

'I feel your sadness, but you're still as beautiful as the day I met you.'

She came over to me and touched my cheek. It was a gesture so familiar to me it made me ache for her. I held her in my arms, feeling the warmth of her breasts beneath her blouse, and I longed for something I knew was gone from her. But I still searched her body for the memory that sustained me like the heat from an ember in a fire.

'I can't feel pleasure any more, Shepherd. I need permission to do so.'

'Is pleasure about permission?'

'I'm buried alive in my grief. If I allow myself desire it feels as though I'm raping my own heart.'

'Denying yourself won't bring Felton back.'

'No one will take his place.'

'No.'

I took her by the hand, and we went upstairs. We undressed in the twilit bedroom, and I touched her and tasted her mouth and recalled that time all those years ago by the well when her face was full of sexual joy. And I caught a glimmer of it in her eyes as I entered her on our marriage bed, then it faded from sight. And while my wife still gave me pleasure, it was tinged with loss and heartache and we felt hollow and alone afterwards. She rose from the bed and stood by the window that looked out onto our back garden and the fields beyond it. Through the crack in the curtains, moonlight caressed her buttocks and the small of her back, as if secretly acknowledging her beauty. A sense of waste howled inside me as I thought of how Mary viewed her beauty as redundant now, a vanity in conflict with her grief.

'We will only ever have one child,' she said.

'I know.'

I went downstairs and locked up the house. I felt I was locking us in with our grief, and I wondered whose way was better, mine, searching for the role of protector when I hadn't been able to protect my son, or Mary's, containing her grief alone. The air felt like ice when I stood near the window.

I went upstairs to the bathroom, past Felton's room. The door was always shut, and we rarely went in there. The last time I'd entered his room I'd found Mary on the floor holding one of his shirts. She was sobbing like a broken child, and the room smelt of mothballs and dead air.

She was sleeping when I returned to our bedroom. I climbed into bed next to her and shut my eyes and saw Maxwell alone in the white forest. He opened his mouth to say something to me, and I fell into the intense blackness between his lips.

* * *

Snow fell in the night. Two feet of it carpeted the landscape and produced the accompanying hush that made our house seem more distant from the road.

When I got up Mary was making coffee. Its smell reached me on the upstairs landing, and I went downstairs feeling hungry.

She made me eggs and bacon, toast and grape jam, and as I ate I thought how Maxwell of all people would benefit from hunting. His survival seemed to hinge on the thing that killed my son. And his choice not to hunt came from a deep moral conviction. Mary and he were alike, their solitude stemmed from the same principles.

Snow continued to fall all morning. By eleven it stood at four feet. I got ready to visit Holly and the girls, taking my winter coat out of the cupboard.

Mary was downstairs when I went to say good-bye. She was washing dishes and turned as I entered the kitchen.

'Let him come and stay here,' she said.

'You mean Maxwell?'

She nodded.

'You say he's a chef?'

'That's what he told me.'

'You know I don't like to cook anymore; he can cook for us if we give him lodging while the cold is in.'

'Are you sure?'

'It seems wrong to leave a grieving young man out in this weather.'

'I think you'll like him.'

'We have a spare room that's never used.'

'If you change your mind, I'll ask him to leave.'

'I wouldn't want another hunting accident on our doorstep.'

'I hope he's still there.'

I walked over to her and kissed her on the cheek and then I left. I drove to Holly's first, remembering that she still didn't have her car and might need help shovelling the snow.

It was banked high outside their house, and they were all out with shovels. I felt guilty as I got out and helped them. I told myself they were my responsibility, not some young man I didn't know. But as I spent the next few hours with them I kept thinking of him out in the forest alone, possibly starving, and I questioned my hesitation. Guilt locked itself into my heart like a broken bone snapping into place.

I drove Holly and the girls into Stowe for some errands. Holly made us turkey sandwiches, and we ate them in her warm kitchen.

Marigold and Joyce looked so fresh-faced and young that day. I thought of their futures and how wrong it was that a man as young as Maxwell should have none beyond what the wilderness had to provide. By the time I left the snow was even thicker. I drove to the forest and parked my pickup.

It took me longer to reach the clearing, and when I got there the light was growing dim. Maxwell was standing by a tree. He had his hands deep in his pockets and was shivering. I walked over to him and offered him my coat. But he shook his head.

'You can't stay out here,' I said.

'You don't need to worry about me.'

'How will you get food if this weather continues?'

'The snow might ease off.'

'I came to offer you a place to stay.'

'No need for that.'

'I spoke to my wife about you, and we both want you to stay with us.'

'That's real generous of you, but I don't feel I can accept it.'

'You'd be doing us a favour. Mary doesn't like to cook anymore.'

'You want me to make your meals?'

'We give you a room, and you can be a chef again.'

'I think my place is out here.'

'You think that's what Anna Belle would want?'

He looked at the pure white ground. Snowflakes settled on his eyelashes.

'No, I don't reckon she would.'

'Come on, my pickup's not far from here.'

'Maybe just until the snow stops.'

'You don't want to spend another night out here.'

'Thank you.'

He gathered up his few things, and I helped him carry them to the road. He was weak and had to keep stopping.

I helped him inside and turned on the engine. I drove him to our house, and he shivered all the way there.

4.

Mary was laying out the plates for supper when we walked through the door. She paused with one poised mid-air and stared out into the hall. Then she put the plate down and came out to us. She ran her eyes down Maxwell's ragged clothes.

'There's a fire in here,' she said. 'And some food on its way.'

'Thank you, Ma'am. I believe you must be Mary.'

She shook his hand.

'Can I take your coat, Maxwell?'

'If it's all the same to you, Ma'am, I'll keep it on a little longer.'

'On one condition.'

'Yes, Ma'am?'

'You stop calling me Ma'am.'

He followed her through to the kitchen and stood by the crackling fire in which splinters of wood rose from a splitting log. After a few minutes he took off his coat. He stood there for some time warming his hands and rubbing his legs through his corduroys while I helped Mary finish laying the table. I glanced at her as I did, and she held my gaze with a look that told me she was pleased with the decision we'd made.

Then we ate her chicken stew. Maxwell was ravenous

and tried to slow down, but he finished before us and sat there looking uncomfortable.

'Would you like some more?' Mary said.

'That was one of the best dishes I've ever eaten. I better let it sit a while.'

'Shepherd tells me you're a chef.'

'That was what I used to do.'

'Then I'm flattered you enjoyed my dish.'

'I didn't realise how cold I was until I got in here and felt the warmth of your fire. I have to thank you for your hospitality.'

'The stew will warm you up.'

'I think I will have a little more.'

'There's apple pie for dessert with Ben & Jerry's ice cream.'

After we ate, we sat and had coffee in the living room.

'It's real kind of you taking me in like this,' Maxwell said. 'I caught a glimpse of myself in the mirror over there just now, and I don't feel fit for civilised company.'

'Oh hush,' Mary said.

'I didn't use to look this way before it all happened.'

'Shepherd told me about your tragedy. Do you have family, Maxwell?' Mary said.

'None now. My daddy died some years ago, and my mother left when I was little. My brother was killed in the Gulf War.'

'Where did you grow up?'

'In Lebanon, New Hampshire.'

'Do you want to go back there?'

'I left years ago. I trained as a chef in Boston where I

worked and where it all happened.'

'You mean the murder of your fiancée?'

Maxwell nodded.

'Nothing felt the same again after that, and so I took off.'

It was strange sitting there listening to Mary talk to him. It reminded me of the way she used to talk to Felton.

It was clear Maxwell was exhausted, and so we showed him to the spare room downstairs next to the small bathroom. Mary had put fresh sheets on the bed and an extra blanket.

'We'll leave you to get some rest,' she said.

'Thank you again, both of you.'

Mary and I cleaned up the dishes. Then we went to bed. As I passed his door on my way upstairs he was reading the Bible.

When I lay down, Mary touched my arm. I kissed her and caressed her breasts beneath her nightie. Then she took me inside her.

That night Mary was passionate in a way she hadn't been since we lost Felton. And I was back by the well with her in my arms on a summer morning long ago.

5.

The next morning when I rose I found Maxwell in the kitchen. A fresh pot of coffee sat on the table. I could see that he'd washed, his hair was a sandy colour, and after a night's rest his eyes looked clearer. He'd used the razor I left for him to shave. Without his beard he looked ten years younger, and his face was flushed with an innocence that summoned a paternal instinct in me.

'Morning, Shepherd,' he said.

'Did you sleep well?'

'Best night I've had in years.'

'After breakfast I want to take you into Stowe to buy you some clothes.'

'I can't allow that.'

'Those aren't going to last much longer.'

He looked down at his threadbare pants and the long strand of cotton that dangled from one leg and laughed.

Maxwell made us scrambled eggs and waffles for breakfast. The eggs tasted soft and moist with a hint of Cabot cheddar. The waffles were sweet and wholesome, and the honey I dripped onto them came from a local Vermont farm.

We went into Stowe, and Mary helped pick out some clothes for him in Shaw's General Store. We got him two of each, pants, shirts, T-shirts, sweaters, and shoes, together with enough underwear and socks to keep him warm. It was clear Maxwell was uncomfortable with the arrangement. He kept looking at his feet and blushing, while Tom, the manager, whom I'd known for many years, glanced his way.

As he packed up our purchases, Tom said to me, 'A relative of yours?'

'No, he's staying with us.'

'I don't think I've seen him before.'

'I found him in the forest living rough; he was nearly starving. We're putting him up for a few days.'

'That's generous of you.'

'Well, he's going to cook for us. He's a chef.'

'Is that right?'

I took the bags, and we went back to the house.

Maxwell changed into his new clothes, and looking at him you wouldn't have guessed the way he'd been living. He began to make preparations for supper.

I left to visit Holly as the snow began to fall again.

I noticed a Chrysler parked on her drive as I drew up. She was waiting for me in the kitchen together with Marigold and Joyce and a young man I didn't know. He had his arm resting on the back of Marigold's chair, and I figured him to be her boyfriend. I'd never known her to go out with a boy, and I felt a sense of vertigo, as if my resources for offering the advice a father might give were lacking.

'Shepherd, this is Owen,' Holly said.

'Pleased to me you,' I said.

Owen stood up, and I shook his hand.

I saw Joyce nudge her sister and giggle, then dart a glance at Owen. He was a good-looking young man. I figured him to be in his early twenties. He had a good bearing, strong physique, open features, and an honest face. I was relieved that I liked him and wondered if he would get on with Maxwell.

'How about some coffee?' Holly said.

'Sounds good.'

I sat down and talked to Owen. He was a ski instructor in Stowe, and he'd been seeing Marigold for some weeks. Both my nieces listened intently without saying a word, and I felt suddenly as if I was interviewing him for a position. And I realised I'd never give any consideration to the romantic aspects of their lives as maturing young women.

'Shepherd will you join us for lunch?' Holly said.

'Do I smell turkey?'

'You do. Owen brought it and took us shopping, my car's ready tomorrow.'

'I'd love to.'

We felt like a family as we ate. The turkey was lean and moist. We had it with cranberry sauce, potatoes, and squash.

'We'd love to see Mary some time,' Holly said.

'I'm sure she'd like that too. Right now she's at the house with our guest.'

'You have someone staying?'

'I found a young man in the forest the other day. He was living rough and told me a heart-wrenching story.'

'Oh?'

I put my knife and fork down.

'His fiancée was murdered.'

'That's terrible.'

'He said the man who did it walked free and he lost everything. He'd gone into the wilderness to come to terms with his loss and to try to forgive the killer.'

'That's quite remarkable. And you say he's staying with you?'

'He's in the spare room and almost didn't accept my offer. He's well brought up and religious. When the snow began to fall I worried for him. So I went back out to where I found him. He was starving and freezing. He worked as a chef, and the way I got him to come and stay with us was for him to cook.'

'What does he look like?' Joyce said.

'When I found him he looked rough, he hadn't washed for days, and he was wearing rags. I bought him some clothes, and after his shower this morning he'd shaved. He's a handsome man, and you can tell he's had his share of pain in this world, but there's something unusual about him.'

'Unusual how?' Joyce said.

'I think it's the religion. His only possessions are a few pans and a Bible.'

'That's all he's got?'

'What's with all the questions Joyce?' Holly said.

'Just asking.'

'It's OK,' I said. 'It's an interesting subject.'

'I think it's really kind of you,' Marigold said. 'What's his name?'

'Maxwell Heed.'

'What does Mary think about it?' Holly said.

'She's taken to him.'

'You know, Shepherd, it could be good for Mary to have someone there. I think although she needs to be on her own, she can't go on living like that forever, it's not her character. I remember how often she used to come and visit us.'

'I think she and Maxwell are alike; they've both sought

solitude to deal with their grief.'

'Then maybe it will help her having him around.'

I stayed for most of the afternoon, and by the time I left, I felt assured that Owen was good company for Marigold. He was polite and respectful, and I felt he would behave around my niece. I drove back home, and when I opened the door I caught the first smell of Maxwell's cooking. The odour was rich and warming. He was in the kitchen, and the table was laid for supper.

'I've roasted some beef; it'll be ready in an hour,' he said.

I watched the snow fall outside the window and felt relieved he was staying with us.

Upstairs Mary was getting out of the shower. I found her wrapped in a towel. I kissed her and smelt roses and summer peaches on her skin, then I held her in my arms. After she dressed we went downstairs, and I opened a bottle of red wine and poured three glasses.

Over a long supper Maxwell told us more of his life.

'I worked for some of the best restaurants in Boston and Cape Cod. I enjoyed the work,' he said. 'But as I say, when I lost it all I saw no reason to stay there and living rough gave me comfort. I found it hard to be among people.'

'I understand that,' Mary said.

'I read my Bible. I try to forgive. But I still see the bullet wounds on Anna Belle. I found her lying on the sofa coated in blood. And I still see that man's laughing face as he left the court house.'

'Who was the man who did it?'

'I can hardly bring myself to talk of him.'

'Then you don't have to.'

There was an awkward silence in which the scraping of cutlery on plates seemed unnaturally loud.

'How were the girls?' Mary said.

'They're well. Holly asked after you, and Marigold has a boyfriend.'

'A boyfriend?'

'Called Owen. I think Holly wanted me to meet him. I got a good sense about him. I told them about Maxwell.'

And so we talked into the evening and avoided asking him about the man who killed Anna Belle. The snow had claimed the landscape when we went to bed.

6.

The following week I drove Maxwell over to meet Holly and the girls. Mary came with us.

They greeted Maxwell warmly. My sister made some lunch for us, a side of ham and salad. And Maxwell blended in as if he'd always been there.

'Maxwell, how are you finding Vermont?' Holly said.

'I guess you could say it reminds me of New Hampshire, where I grew up.'

'Shepherd tells me you worked in Boston.'

'I did for many years.'

'And you're a chef?'

'That's right. Perhaps you and Marigold and Joyce would like to come over one day and I can cook for you all.'

'We'd love to,' Marigold said.

'What will you make us?' Joyce said.

'Well, what would you like?'

'I like most things, generally.'

'Generally,' Marigold said, teasingly. 'You never use that word, all grown up.'

Maxwell was respectful and kind to my nieces, and for the first time I saw them through a stranger's eyes. I thought how pretty and unworldly they were, and I feared for their futures.

I noticed a difference in Marigold's behaviour I couldn't define until Owen arrived. When he walked in I realised she'd been gently flirting with Maxwell, who hadn't responded but behaved discreetly. As she kissed Owen on the cheek, she glanced at Maxwell. He was talking to Joyce and didn't notice.

Owen was at first guarded with him but relaxed as they talked. Suddenly that afternoon Marigold seemed to me to be older than Joyce by many years. I'd never witnessed her display her feminine charms the way she did with both young men. And Maxwell behaved entirely correctly.

When we left, Holly said to me, 'He's a fine person.'

'I believe he is.'

We were standing by the kitchen door and Maxwell, Mary, Marigold, Joyce, and Owen were outside. And I caught a glimpse of a family tableau and felt we were all connected by some common goodness. That picture has faded over the years and become corrupted by other images. We never seem to think the things we don't know about can do us harm.

7.

Every day we enjoyed dishes that were the mark of a fine chef. Our lives became punctuated by a rhythm of smells and flavours that rose from the kitchen and imbued the house with the feeling of a home again. We were being nourished by a stranger, and it felt as if I'd known him for years. One evening over supper I asked him about his beliefs, remembering what he'd said to me in the forest.

'I went into the wilderness to forgive the man who killed Anna Belle. I believe forgiveness is the ultimate lesson for a man.'

'But can you really do that?' Mary said. 'I don't know who killed Felton, but I can't forgive what he did, he never even owned up to it.'

'We misunderstand what forgiveness is.'

'And what do you think it is?'

'Understanding the nature of man.'

'Understanding what drove Anna Belle's killer to do what he did?' I said.

'Yes.'

'Isn't that justifying what he did?'

'Not entirely. It means knowing what man is and that I am a man and I must forgive, to cleanse me of hatred and thoughts of revenge.'

'We both suffer from a sense of injustice,' Mary said.

'And there is no justice,' Maxwell said, 'at least not where Anna Belle's killer is concerned. Some men enter our lives to test us, to show us hidden aspects of our being.'

A shadow passed across his face then, and he looked down at the table.

'Felton was shot by accident,' Mary said, 'I've tried to understand what drove the man who caused it to hide from his crime. He must have known, even if not at the time, he must have read about it in the papers. But to enter the mind of a man who deliberately kills is another thing entirely. I would be afraid of being corrupted.'

'That's what a man like him would want.'

'Wouldn't you be in danger of becoming like him if you really understood him?' I said.

'Forgiveness removes any corruption that Anna Belle's murder may have produced in me.'

'I'll never know who shot Felton,' Mary said.

'Maybe one day you will.'

'Knowing who killed Anna Belle is no comfort to you.'

'None at all where the man who did it is concerned. I've never told you about him.'

'No, Maxwell,' I said.

'Perhaps it's time I did. It's something you ought to hear, and I fear I've misled you.'

'Misled us?' I said.

'There was another reason behind my choice to live wild, and that is I fear Anna Belle's killer is coming after me, he made threats to do so. I sometimes ask myself whether I was out there trying to forgive or running away, and I really don't know, it seemed the only place for me to be.'

'Do you really think he's after you?' Mary said.

'The day I saw him laughing in the court house I knew what he was.' Maxwell's eyes looked like emeralds burning in a fire, and his face was white as he spoke. 'His name is Temple Jones, and he's capable of anything. He'd followed Anna Belle; he likes women who have an innocent type of beauty. He raped her before he killed her.'

'Good God. And he walked free?' Mary said.

'He hired some fancy lawyer who tore the case apart. The police had made mistakes.'

'Sooner or later justice will catch up with him,' I said.

'He spoke to me when he was leaving court. I was standing outside shaking after the verdict, and he walked past me and stopped. I'm going to tell you what he said. I don't mean to shock you, but I want you to know the kind of man Temple Jones is, in case he is following me. Forgive me for some of the language I'm about to use, they're his words, not mine.'

He hesitated and looked at Mary.

'It's OK, Maxwell,' she said, 'I've heard bad language before.'

'I'll never forget his words. And he said it all with laughter in his voice. "She tasted real sweet," he said. "I bet she never did the things for you she did for me before I stabbed the whore, but then women like her kind always hide their real desires. Did she make that little chirping noise for you? She tasted like cherry pie when I put my tongue inside her. I made her come. Then I watched her beg. I told her I'd save her life if she did it for me, I lied. I owe no favours to a whore like her. When I stabbed her she was calling for her mother, she never mentioned you. By the way, I plan to do me some more. If you mention this conversation to anyone, I'll come after you and violate anyone you love or who loves you. I hate purity, it's a disease. Take Christianity, founded on the lie of a pregnant virgin, now who's done more harm, Christians or me?" As he stood there I couldn't speak, he filled my head with those images. I collapsed after he left, fell into a fever for days. I ran from him and what he did. I truly believe Temple Jones is capable of anything.'

Mary drew her cardigan around her.

'What a despicable man,' she said.

'I did mention the conversation to the police, and that's why I fear he's following me. I saw him once standing at the corner of my road smiling, shortly before I left.'

'How would he find you out here?' I said.

'That I don't know, but I thought it right to warn you.'

'Warn us?'

'Shepherd, you've taken me in, and as I began to feel stronger I realised you may have placed yourself in jeopardy. I don't want to expose others to the danger I may be in.'

'Unless he's followed you through the wilderness, there's no way he could find you here,' I said.

'But that's the thing; it's as if he has. I used to think I saw him hiding behind trees in the snow, waiting.'

'You were probably light-headed from hunger and seeing things,' Mary said.

'I needed to tell you in case you wanted me to leave.'

'Wanted you to leave? Of course not,' Mary said.

'Not at all,' I said.

'I apologise for the things I told you; it's best in many ways not to speak of him at all. It's as if when I do I feel his presence, as if he's trying to take me over in some way. If I ever see him here or believe he's found me I'll disappear. If you ever return to find I'm gone without a word it's because

I've had to.'

'Maxwell, I don't believe this man knows where you are,' I said.

'I hope you're right. But just in case you're wrong I'll describe him to you. He stands at about my height, is medium built but strong. He's hard to describe beyond that, as if his features are nondescript, but he laughs at you when he talks to you. There were many times I tried to recall his features when I was living rough, and they seemed to fade from my mind. I believe if he turned up here he would try to harm you. That's why I stayed outdoors, to make sure he didn't know where I am. Shepherd, if I'd told this to you out in the forest maybe you wouldn't have taken me in.'

'It would have made no difference,' I said.

'How long did you live like that?' Mary said.

'Many months, I lost track of time.'

'And how long is it since Anna Belle was killed?' Mary said.

'Over a year now.'

'Then I honestly believe there is no way this man can find you or is looking for you,' I said.

'I hope you're right.'

'He was just playing games. What did the police say when you reported what he said to you?'

'That they'd speak to him. That's when I left.'

'You're safe here,' I said.

'He said other things after the trial when he spoke to me that showed he'd been watching Anna Belle. He mentioned some of her personal habits, and I used to wonder how long he'd had her under surveillance before he killed her. I think he'd been staking out other women, too. Temple Jones likes to pick a certain kind of woman. He said he likes to test their purity, especially the ones that pretend they're not corrupt. But he watches them first, he always watches them first.'

The conversation had disturbed Maxwell, and we went to bed shortly after that. I lay down to sleep but found myself getting up to check I'd locked the front and back doors.

8.

The following week Holly and the girls came to lunch. Maxwell cooked a steak and vegetable stew. The meat was tender, and the sauce was rich. The rutabaga and the potatoes tasted of the wholesome Vermont soil that bore them. Maxwell had folded flavour upon flavour into the dish. And it tasted pure and fresh.

Mary and Holly talked about the winter coming on. The temperature was dropping on a daily basis, and I believed its severity would have been too much for Maxwell to survive. He seemed at ease and content living with us.

It was after lunch that I witnessed an interesting incident. Maxwell was clearing up, and Marigold was helping set the dishes on the side. He was rinsing a plate when she came up behind him. I noticed she brushed against him and paused, pressing her breasts into his shoulder. Maxwell simply carried on with his task.

I'd never seen Marigold behave like that. As I turned round, Joyce was standing behind me watching her sister.

Holly and Mary talked a long time, and I felt we'd all once again do things together. As we sat there talking we heard some hunters' guns go off. For a moment I saw Mary's face change, then she resumed her conversation.

Maxwell stole a glance at her, to see if the noise had disturbed her. Then he carried on talking to Joyce and Marigold.

And I thought about the past, of Felton, of the hole in my heart, of wounds we cannot see. I watched them, my nieces, my guest, sister, and wife, and I wondered if my fear of the future where my nieces was concerned was really only my blocked past. Was I distancing myself from my agony over Felton? Was I a tourist in my own heart?

9.

The red barn at Holly's house had a distinct character for each season. In the spring wild flowers decorated the ground outside it, and when you stepped inside, the winter chill it had held for the preceding months was fading and being replaced by a gentle warmth. By summer, morning glory and the cypress vine my sister cultivated with her able hands climbed the rotting wood. In fall its rose colour seemed a part of the red landscape, a statement of its place in Vermont. Then winter came round again, and it stood there on the snow, the only colour you could see from Holly's house, a promise of more summers.

We once had a picnic by the barn on a July afternoon. All of us gathered at a table Felton and I lugged from the house. Mary wore a summer dress with a pattern of flowers. Holly served us loaded potato salad and cold ham, garden salad, and warm slices of homemade bread. Marigold and Joyce were young that day that exists many years ago and is swathed in colour in my memory. We existed before purity was scarred, we dwelt in a heartland I hear like a distant song now. It was a day when our security was assured, and we were unaware of the lie that was. We weren't arrogant but unaware of things that no one wants to know. I see us there, seated at the table, picnicking by the barn. We are full of colour, the food and the company part of a painting. Flowers climb across Mary's dress, and I ache for her femininity.

We are pure even in desire. The food is wholesome, fetched from the good soil. The barn watches over us.

But the scene lacks the colour of the barn in the fall. Recalling that almost breaks my heart. For while the cold would take hold, the different shades of red and gold lied about the coming winter. And I often wonder now if it is those lies, comforting and alluring, that we seek in solace from the storm.

None of us wanted to go into the barn in winter. But it remained there, solidly red on the landscape, a constant amid seasonal change. It is rust-coloured now and still holds warmth in its flaking paint and weathered wood. Its resistance to collapse challenges me. It still appeals to passing tourists, an image of quaintness they take away to other lives. It is the house of memories, a fragile structure that offers permanency. It has been the scene of quite different pleasures.

10.

A few days later we all visited Holly. I sensed tension between Marigold and Owen. We were all sitting in the kitchen when he laid his arm on her shoulder and she stood up and walked over to the wood burning stove.

'We're nearly out of kindling,' she said.

'I'll go and fetch some from the barn,' Owen said.

He began to walk towards the door, but Marigold put her hand up.

'I've done it before, you stay here.'

He flushed and glanced at Maxwell as he sat down.

The bracing air took some heat out of the kitchen as Marigold stepped outside.

I wondered if Maxwell had noticed the look Owen gave him, but he was engaged in conversation with Joyce and seemed as familiar to her as if he'd been her brother.

'Are you going to carry on living with Uncle Shepherd and Aunt Mary?' she said.

'Just till the winter's out.'

'Then what?'

'I guess I'll move on.'

'Move on where?'

'I don't rightly know.'

'You can't just wander off.'

'Shepherd and Mary have been really kind putting me up, but I don't want to outstay my welcome.'

'How do you feel, Uncle Shepherd?'

'I can't imagine Maxwell being unwelcome in our house.'

'There you go,' Joyce said, nudging him with her elbow.

Just then we heard Marigold scream, then there was a crash from the barn.

'That sounded like falling wood,' Holly said.

I got up, but Maxwell was already opening the door. We all went outside to the barn, Owen running ahead of us, but Maxwell got there first. I watched him vanish through the open door.

When I got there I saw the cougar. It was standing two feet from Marigold, who was at the back of the barn next to the collapsed wood pile. She had a piece of timber in her hands and was holding it out in front of her. The cougar was thin and snarling, his ears flattened.

Mary and Joyce had stopped at the entrance. Holly was standing next to me with her hand on her mouth. Owen stood frozen behind Maxwell, who was inching forward.

'I wish we had a gun,' Joyce said.

I watched as Maxwell gained on the cougar. Then it moved in for Marigold, who swung the wood at it. Maxwell jammed his knee into the cougar's back and wrapped his hands around its throat and began to choke it. The cougar writhed, tried to fling him off, but Maxwell held on. Eventually some of the fight went out of the cougar and Maxwell let go. The cat turned and snarled, but Maxwell raised both his arms and growled at it, like a bear in the wild would. The cat glanced over at us then ran out of the barn through the opening at the side where a plank of wood had come loose.

Marigold dropped the piece of wood and threw her arms around Maxwell's neck as Owen looked away. I walked over to them.

'Are you hurt?' I said to her.

'No, I was picking up the wood when I saw it. I pushed the pile over to scare it off.'

'You were awesome,' Joyce said to Maxwell.

'No need for guns, use nature to fight nature,' he said.

We went back to the house and watched the fire die as Maxwell returned to the barn to get more wood. I noticed Owen's car was gone as Maxwell stoked up the fire.

Holly went over to him and took his hands in hers.

'Thank you for saving my daughter's life.'

'I've come across wild cats in the woods before.'

'Maxell, I don't know how to thank you,' Marigold said.

'I couldn't just stand by and let you become cat food, could I?'

'We need to fix that plank,' Holly said.

'I'll see to that,' Maxwell said.

I went outside with him and helped him fix the gap in the side of the barn.

'There's a paw mark here,' he said. 'Looks like the cougar saw it was loose and pushed it open.'

We used eight inch nails and drove them deep into the wood. Then we piled the collapsed kindling back up.

Holly had some clam chowder on the stove when we went back inside, and we ate it steaming hot with walnut bread.

'You see, I think you're needed here,' Joyce said to Maxwell. 'You can't just wander off.'

11.

I didn't ask about what happened between Marigold and Owen, but the next time I saw them together it was clear she was angry with him. Every time he came close to her she'd move away or engage in conversation with Maxwell. Marigold was asking Maxwell about his life, careful to avoid mentioning his tragedy, and as I looked at her I thought how she was exactly the kind of woman Temple Jones would prey on, beautiful and pure.

'I don't know how you survived, living rough,' Marigold said.

'It's not that hard if you know how.'

'Didn't you miss human company?'

'Oh yes.'

'Well I'm so glad Uncle Shepherd found you.'

'And so am I.'

'You feel like one of the family.'

'Well, Marigold, I'm honoured.'

As he said it there was a shadow on his face.

I watched them talk, and while I could see that Marigold was attracted to Maxwell, he showed no sexual interest in her, as if he was her brother. And I thought how strange it was, that this good man had been so lost and that I'd found him. Since I had, Mary had changed. It was as if that maternal part of her that had withered had begun to grow again.

We returned home late. Then we spent a quiet evening. When I went to bed Maxwell was staring out of the window of his room. I said good night to him, but he didn't respond.

12.

The next morning I went into Stowe. Maxwell hadn't got up, which was unusual for him, and when I returned it was late morning and his door was still shut.

'Do you think he's sick?' I said to Mary.

'I don't know. I didn't want to disturb him.'

I opened his door and peered inside. The bed was made, the curtains drawn, and there was a note on the bed.

Dear Shepherd and Mary,

I saw Temple Jones in the road last night, and I've left because no one is safe if he's tailing me. Thank you for all your hospitality.

Maxwell

I showed the note to Mary. He'd taken one set of clothes I'd bought him and left the others neatly folded on the bed.

'How will he survive in this cold?' she said.

'I'll go and look for him.'

'I'm sure that man can't have followed him here.'

'He obviously thinks he has.'

'It's his grief.'

'He's trying to protect us.'

I drove to the forest and went to the clearing where I'd first seen Maxwell, but it was empty and covered with snow. I walked for miles and found no tracks at all except those of deer. When I finally returned it was growing dark and I was hungry and tired. Mary made me a cheese sandwich, and I ate it and drank a whisky to steady my nerves. I was deeply worried that Maxwell wouldn't survive the night, not because of Temple Jones but the severe temperature.

Just then the phone rang.

'Uncle Shepherd, it's Marigold, did I leave my house keys there?'

'No, I don't think so.'

I cradled the phone between my shoulder and neck and asked Mary if she'd seen Marigold's keys. She shook her head.

'We'll take a look and tell you if they turn up,' I said.

She must have heard the strain in my voice, because she said, 'Are you all right?'

'Maxwell has disappeared. He left a note, and he's gone.'

'Why would he do that?'

'It's a long story.'

'Where do you think he is?'

'Right now my guess would be the forest.'

After I hung up, Mary and I spent half an hour looking for Marigold's keys but didn't find them. I never for a moment believed Temple Jones was a real threat.

13.

The next morning after breakfast I went out looking for him again. I was driving to the forest when Tom passed me in his car. He slowed and rolled down his window.

'I've just seen that young man who was staying with you,' he said.

'Where?'

'In my barn, he'd slept there the night.'

'Is he still there?'

'No. That was about an hour ago, he never said a word to me when I asked him what he was doing there, he just wandered off.'

'Do you mind if I go and take a look?'

'Be my guest, but as I say, he's not there. He looked strange, different.'

'If you see him, will you call me?'

'Sure.'

I was relieved Maxwell had found a warm place for the night, and as I drove there I hoped he might still be in the vicinity and that I could talk him out of his fear.

I opened the doors to the barn and looked around. There were no signs of his presence, and I went into the surrounding woods. But I couldn't see any footprints at all. Maxwell must have walked in the tire tracks of Tom's car and gone into the woods from there.

I spent the entire morning looking for him. I checked the forest. I drove along the mountain roads hoping to spot him. Eventually I returned for lunch, feeling as if I'd lost my son again.

When I did, I found a broken cup lying on the kitchen floor. I could hear a noise upstairs.

14.

The noise was coming from the bathroom. When I got to the landing I could hear running water, and I opened the door. Mary was standing in the shower. When she saw me she screamed, then stopped, as she registered it was me. She was scrubbing at her body with a hard brush, her skin was pink, and her lower abdomen was bleeding. I could see the brush marks on it, and as I stood there my heart felt like a broken stone sinking into a cold well. I got her out of the shower and put a towel round her.

'He came here, Shepherd, to our house,' she said.

'Who?'

'That man, the one Maxwell talked about.'

'Temple Jones?'

'Yes.'

'Has he hurt you?'

'Yes.'

'What did he do?'

'I was washing up the dishes when I felt him.'

'He attacked you.'

'He speaks in a cold whisper, like ice. He said, "Maxwell's gone, Temple's here."' He had his hands around my throat, and he said, "I like them young but I like them like you, too." He strangled me with one hand and ran his other hand inside my dress and touched me. I felt sick, and I kept looking in the window to try to see his face.'

'I'm going to get my gun and kill him.'

'You won't find him.'

'I will.'

'He hasn't got a face. He's deformed; he has a mouth and nothing else.'

'You're in shock.'

'I know what I saw.'

'You need to get dressed. Then you need to see a doctor.'

'I don't want to see anyone, except Felton.'

'Are you injured?'

'You know what he said then? "It was real good of you, Mary, to put up Maxwell, you and Shepherd."'

'He must have been watching us.'

'I told him I didn't know where Maxwell is, he said, "I do. I came here to defile you before I do other things." Then he did something I'll never forget.'

'I need to call the police.'

'Shepherd, he reached behind me and picked up a kitchen knife. It was the knife Maxwell used to use to chop vegetables with. I'd made a salad before he came in. I'd chopped some tomatoes and lettuce and was washing a cup when he entered our home and violated me. He took the knife and reached between my legs. I tried fighting him, but he held the blade to my throat. Then he said, "I'm going to put this inside you. If you behave, I won't hurt you, if you don't, I'll cut your womanhood till it's nothing more than a ragged red ribbon." Then he put the handle inside me. He said, "You're fortunate I used the friendly end as I like to call it; many women get the other side."'

'I'm going to find this man.'

'He pushed it inside me and leaned across and took some salad. He put some in my mouth as he raped me with the knife.'

'My God.'

'Who have we let into our house?'

'This is not Maxwell's fault.'

'He's not Felton; you should never have put him up.'

I helped Mary get dressed, and then I took her downstairs to the living room and gave her a brandy. I poured one for myself and phoned the police.

I knew she shouldn't have washed and that she'd destroyed any forensic evidence, but I wanted everyone hunting Temple Jones the way he'd hunted Maxwell down. As I made the call, my head was filled with the desire to take the law into my own hands.

The police came and spoke to Mary. They took her description of her attacker and listened to my account of how we'd put Maxwell up and what he told us of Temple Jones.

I could see their hesitation as she spoke of her faceless attacker, but they said nothing. Then they took us to Stowe police station. Mary was examined by a doctor. She hadn't sustained any internal injuries. But she'd washed the evidence away.

When we returned home, she went to bed. I made sure the house was locked, and I got my Winchester shotgun out of the cupboard where it had been locked away for years. I cleaned it and loaded it before I joined Mary. I dreamed of killing Temple Jones like a dog, but I couldn't see his eyes and when I squeezed the trigger nothing happened.

15.

When I got up the next day I found Mary sitting with her legs tucked under her in the living room. It was barely daylight, and she said something to me, but I couldn't understand her words. It sounded as though she was coughing through a broken lung. I stayed with her, and I kept seeing the faceless Temple Jones raping her in my house, the house I'd offered as a refuge to Maxwell, who was perhaps that moment being killed by him. All morning my rage fed off my impotence like a blind snake seeking a mate.

At noon I tried making some lunch. Neither of us had eaten all day. I made a ham sandwich and set it in front of Mary with a mug of steaming coffee, but an hour later it remained uneaten. I chewed on mine, but all I tasted was bile.

I tried to think of where Maxwell would go, of how he would survive the weather, and I decided he was using outbuildings.I didn't want to leave Mary alone, but I also wanted to find him before Temple Jones did.

I called Tom and explained to him what had happened. I could hear the shock in his voice.

'I'd be grateful if you could come and stay with Mary for an hour. I need to go somewhere, and I don't want to leave her alone.'

'I'm on my way.'

'Oh, and Tom, bring your gun.'

I told Mary where I was going and to call me on my cell phone if she needed.

'I think I'll go to sleep,' she said.

And so I left her sleeping when Tom arrived. He was sitting in the kitchen drinking coffee with his Colt .45 on the table next to him when I set out to Holly's in the thick snow.

I hoped to find Maxwell in her barn. What I was about to find would change my life and the lives of those around me forever.

16.

All the lights were on at her house. And the front door was open. I got out of my pickup cautiously. I walked towards the house with my Winchester. As I did, I noticed Owen's Chrysler parked at the side of the house. Both the driver's and passenger's doors were open.

I stepped slowly towards the front door. I could see the side of the kitchen table from the front steps, and as I walked in I saw Holly.

She was tied to a chair at the back of the room. She had duct tape digging into her mouth, and her eyes were filled with pain and fear. But there was another expression in them that for a brief second I tried to decipher, but I was too slow to realise what she was trying to tell me. Then I felt the cold muzzle of a rifle placed against the back of my skull, and I heard his voice behind me.

'Put it down Shepherd,' he said in a whisper.

The noise reminded me of fine sand paper being scraped across a stone wall.

I did as he said and slowly laid my shotgun on the table in front of me.

'Put your hands behind your head. Lie on the floor, face down.'

I got to my knees and leaned forward.

'Hands behind your back, wrists together.'

I felt wire being wrapped around them until it cut into my skin.

'Get up,' he said.

I rolled onto my side and tried to prop myself up. I still couldn't see him. I was facing Holly who remained tied to the chair. I managed to get onto one knee and stand with difficulty. Then I turned and saw him. He had the rifle aimed at me.

He was as Mary had described, but he was wearing the mask of a man with a mouth and no other features. The image was obscene. An eyeless face is inhuman. His entire body was covered in a long black trench coat, and the only discernible thing beneath it was a pair of black suede cowboy boots with spurs. I was thankful that Marigold and Joyce weren't there. I thought of Owen's car outside and imagined they'd run for help and perhaps the police were on their way. But that afternoon we were more isolated than I could ever imagine.

'You think I'm going to shoot you?' he said.

'Is that what you've done to Maxwell?'

'Would you like to see Maxwell again?'

'What do you intend to do?'

'A little fun and games.'

'The police are on their way. I called them before I arrived; they know where I am.'

'I don't think so.'

'They're probably heading out here as we speak.'

'Mary tasted real good,' he said. 'I bet she said I raped her, but then whores are all the same, show one thing to their husbands another to the man who creeps into their house at midnight with only a bone in his pants and a knife in his pocket. She moaned low and deep, she ever made that sound for you, Shepherd?'

'You're nothing but a coward.'

He walked over to Holly, the rowels on his spurs clinking on the wooden floor. He reached down and groped one of her breasts. Then he lifted her sweater and ripped open her blouse. I looked away but he pointed the rifle at me.

'I want you to watch. Don't say you never looked at your sister's titties, Shepherd?'

I lowered my eyes.

'Watch or I'll shoot her.'

I pretended to look, but instead I looked past it, at the snow falling outside the window, at the purity of the landscape. But I could still see my sister out of the corner of my eye.

'You know I still don't think you're watching. One more chance or she gets a bullet.'

And so I watched.

He unhooked her bra and touched her. Then he put his hand up her dress.

Holly tried to keep her legs together, but he slapped her. And all the time he kept glancing back at me, making sure I was witnessing his defilement of my sister.

'Nice tits, but not as nice as your two girls I imagine. I reckon they're real sweet and might be persuaded to do all sorts of things for a few bucks. What do you say Shepherd, shall we go and see how good the two nieces taste? Marigold, now there's a whore in the making if ever I saw one. Are they virgins, Holly?'

'You're sick and need to be put down,' I said.

'I'll be putting your nieces down on their backs shortly

and inspecting their insides with my knife, Shepherd. Come on, don't say you never touched their titties when you came to visit them, all them visits for what? Tastes sweet as cherry pie a young bit of pussy, you know what I mean. I can see it in your eyes.'

'If you lay a hand on my nieces, I'll kill you.'

'You know it was real easy finding you. Turn around.'

I did, relieved to look away. Then I heard his footsteps behind me and felt something smash into the back of my head.

17.

When I came to I was gagged and tied to a chair and my head was throbbing. Then a hand grabbed the back of my hair and jerked my head upwards.

'Take a look, Shepherd,' Temple Jones said. 'I'm going to show you what your nieces are made of.'

I was in Holly's barn. Holly was next to me tied to a chair, her blouse open. Some feet in front of me were Marigold and Joyce, gagged with duct tape and tied to kitchen chairs. And there was another figure further off, lying on his side, with a pool of blood by his head and a tire iron next to him. I could see it was Owen.

Temple Jones stepped in front of me. Then he put his rifle down and walked over to Marigold.

Her eyes seemed to belong to someone else as he touched her. As he groped her breasts she produced a choked scream from her throat. Then he removed a long hunting knife from a sheath hanging from his leather belt and cut the front of her sweater open. He unbuttoned her blouse, and I looked down at the dirt.

What happened next was something I will never forget, try how I may. I still bear the scars I made trying to wrench my useless hands free from the wire that lacerated my skin, as my sweating palms filled with my own blood.

Temple Jones came over to me and lifted up my head. He

had the knife in his other hand.

'If you look away, Shepherd, I will blind your sister with the tip of this knife. You will be personally responsible for the loss of her eyesight and may have to recount to her in future years what happened to her daughters this day. A mother's concern will always want to know the things that befall her children in this world.'

I tried to calculate how long I'd been there. I told Tom I'd be back in an hour. But it was impossible to tell what time it was. I told myself the police would arrive before Temple Jones caused more harm. But there was no noise at all, no sirens in the distance. The only sounds were those he produced from the people in that barn.

18.

He walked back to Marigold who was straining against the ropes. Then he cut her free, holding her by the hair with one hand.

'If you don't want me to kill Joyce,' Temple Jones said, 'then strip.'

'How do I know you won't kill us all?'

'You don't.'

Marigold debated for a few moments then turned round.

'Keep your eyes on this bitch, Shepherd,' Temple Jones said.

I watched her back as she pulled off her blouse then her bra, removed her shoes and socks, lowered her jeans and waited.

'The rest,' Temple Jones said.

She pulled down her underwear and stood there shivering.

'Turn round.'

She did, and I looked away.

'Shepherd, you better watch this, or I'm gonna cut her nipples off,' Temple Jones said.

And so I watched.

'I've always hated fresh-faced purity that hides in a whore's heart,' he said. 'Your innocence nauseates me, as does your unworldly smugness.'

His whisper resonated in the barn, as if he was speaking with the assistance of a pressure hose. And he seemed so familiar, this faceless monster, and I thought of Maxwell's description of him, and how it had made him come alive in our living room and our minds all those weeks ago when he'd warned us about him.

Then Temple Jones began to touch her with his free hand, holding the knife in the other one. Marigold batted at him, screamed, tried to move back, but he grabbed her by the neck and pushed her to the ground. He stuck the knife in the dirt next to him.

'If you can impress me with what you can do,' he said. 'You can save them all.'

'What do you want me to do?'

'Show me how much of a whore you are.'

'I'm not a whore.'

'Bashful, are you Marigold? I think you weren't bashful with our dead friend Owen.'

He dragged her by the hair behind the wood we'd stacked the day she was attacked by the cougar. I struggled to get free but succeeded only in cutting myself. Holly hung her head, and Joyce stared out at the open door behind me. I studied her face for a sign that someone had come to rescue us.

When Temple Jones returned with Marigold she was wiping her mouth. Her lip was bleeding.

'I think I just got religion,' Temple Jones said, 'this here young whore took it all in and swallowed hard like she was real thirsty.' He touched the top of her nose. 'Now I don't want you to freeze, so put your clothes back on, but don't bother with your underwear since you won't be needing them with what I have in mind for you.'

Marigold put on her jeans, blouse, sweater, and shoes.

'Now sit,' Temple Jones said.

He tied her back into the chair.

Then he walked over to Joyce and ran the tip of his knife down her cheek. Blood began to weep from the cut.

'I always did have a sweet tooth, got something for me hidden in them jeans of yours, ain't you?'

Joyce was straining against the rope, the veins in her neck protruding as he began to touch her. He kept turning his head in my direction to make sure I was watching. I searched for his eyes beneath the two pinholes in the mask and saw only darkness.

He felt her breasts then put his hand between her legs. Then he cut her clothes from her body. They fell away in strips, first her sweater, then her blouse and jeans. He unhooked her bra. He touched her nipples; then he put his hand down her panties. I watched Marigold struggle against her ropes.

'You paying attention, Uncle Shepherd? You're going to have them next.'

The whole series of events assumed the irrational reality of a dream. I was hypnotised by the horror of it all.

He pulled down Joyce's panties and put his finger inside her. Then he ungagged her.

'Nice little tits and a tight snatch,' he said. 'I'm going to show you what it's made for. Can you do it like your sister does? Or are you a virgin?'

'Please,' Joyce said. 'Why are you doing this?'

'Because I hate the pure, you little whore. It's a living lie I'm here to expose. There's no purity in your heart; you want the rough and ready sex of animals in a field.'

He undid the rope, and as he did Joyce pushed him hard

in the chest, knocking him back, and darted past him towards where Owen lay. She picked up the tire iron, and as Temple Jones gained on her she swung it at him. He ducked, and she caught him a glancing blow on the shoulder. She swung again, and he ducked and caught her arm. He gripped it tightly and pressed his body against her.

'Think you can get away, bitch?'

He cut her arm with his knife, and she dropped the tire iron. Temple Jones kicked it away from them. He held her by the wrist, and Joyce tried to kick him, but he hit her, knocking her to the ground. The he got on top of her and forced her legs apart.

'You want the unfriendly end inserted in you?' he said. 'Mary liked the knife; you're going to enjoy it even more.'

He was holding her head down with one hand as he placed the handle between her legs. Then she clawed at his neck. His back was to me and for a second the mask was pulled away, but I couldn't see his face. He pulled the mask back on and secured it as Joyce scrambled to her feet and ran towards the barn door.

But he came after her, grabbing her by the hair and yanking her back to the ground. He dragged her all the way over to where Marigold sat tied to the chair.

'You two can get it on,' he said. 'How 'bout both sisters put on a show for us?'

But Joyce was hysterical. She struck out at him again, and Temple Jones punched her in the mouth, knocking her to the ground.

Then he leaned over her and stabbed her to death. I vomited into my gag and swallowed the puke and the bile that burned my throat.

To this day I cannot count the amount of times he

punctured her body. He pushed the knife in to the hilt again and again. When he finally stood up Joyce was so badly lacerated I could see her intestines.

Holly was trying to scream behind her gag. Temple Jones walked over to Marigold and undid her ropes.

'Now you and me are going to get it on,' he said. 'Take your clothes off.'

Marigold complied, with the weariness of trauma.

'Get down there on the floor next to your dead sister,' he said.

'No.'

He grabbed her wrist and pulled her over to Holly. Then he slid the end of his knife up Holly's skirt.

'You want me to cut your mother?'

'OK, OK.'

He led Marigold to where Joyce lay. She sat down at the edge of the pool of blood.

'No, in it, bitch,' Temple Jones said.

Marigold edged into the blood.

'Lie back.'

She did slowly, keeping her eyes on the barn door.

Temple Jones had his back to me, so thankfully I couldn't see it all. He reached down with one hand and parted Marigold's legs. He stuck the knife in the dirt beside him and got on top of her. He unzipped his fly. Then he raped her. Marigold screamed once as he entered her and he took her throat in his hand and choked her. For a brief moment, over his rocking shoulder, I saw her face. Her eyes had wandered away from the barn and she'd gone somewhere else, and I don't think she ever returned.

When he finished he stood and zipped up his fly. Marigold

lay there without moving as he turned round.

He came over to me and tore off my gag.

'Want a go, Shepherd? She ain't bad, but I bet Joyce would've been sweeter, all that fight, didn't get her nowhere though.'

'How do you know our names?' I said.

'I met you all.'

'You mean you spied on us.'

'Put on your clothes,' he said to Marigold.

She got to her feet and wandered over to where her clothes lay and dressed. Then Temple Jones tied her arms and feet together.

'You move, and I'll cut you,' he said, pointing the knife at her. 'I think I'll do Holly next, see how she compares to her daughters.'

'If the law doesn't get you, I'm going to kill you,' I said.

'Are you?'

'Untie me and see.'

'Oh I'm going to untie you all right, Shepherd, and when I do you won't know what's real anymore.'

I don't know if it was the extreme shock I was feeling but in that moment it all seemed familiar, as if the scene was frozen in time. His whisper was something I'd heard before. I tried to place it, but I couldn't. And I thought that if I didn't escape he would go after Mary.

'What have you done to Maxwell?' I said.

'Who do you think Maxwell is?'

'The man whose fiancée you killed.'

'He lied to you.'

'About what?'

'Everything, Shepherd, just like you've lied, like your nieces pretended they weren't a pair of no good whores.'

'You just killed a virgin, you're insane.'

'You don't even know who I am.'

'I don't want to.'

'Oh but you do. Want to know who's behind this mask, Shepherd? Come on say you don't and lie again, maybe I'll kill Holly next, or Marigold.'

'Why do you talk in a whisper?'

There was no whisper to what he said next. As he spoke I froze. I knew the voice. My horror that afternoon was about to deepen.

'You're a charitable fool, but then again I call your charity your guilt,' he said.

Temple Jones removed the mask. And Maxwell stood there staring down at me.

'You see who Temple Jones is?'

'You, why?'

'You don't know, you really don't know?'

'I put you up. I found you freezing.'

'I knew you'd come along that day, you often take that walk. I'd been watching you. Temple Jones always watches those he decides to visit. I only lived out there a day until you came and invited me to your house and wife. Mary is a fine woman. I think I'll go pay her a visit and have a piece of her snatch after I finish here. Maybe I'll try a bit of gentle buggery and home cooking. Or maybe I'll just cut her to ribbons.'

'Why have you done this to us?'

'Maxwell Heed was Temple Jones's invention.'

'I wish I'd left you starving in that forest. I wish the hunters had shot you.'

'Too late for that, Shepherd, you handed me your wife and nieces.'

'You cooked for us. Why didn't you finish us off then?'

'Because I wanted to get to know you. I was a chef, that part is true, in the army.'

'And the story about Anna Belle?'

'I made her up. But there are plenty of women like her I done worse things to.'

'How did you know I'd put you up?'

But I never heard his answer. In that moment Marigold somehow wrestled her legs free of the ropes and ran past him.

Temple Jones sprinted after her. I waited, dreading what he would do next. I looked at Holly who stared blankly ahead. Several minutes seemed to pass.

Then he came back with Marigold. He had his fist clenched in her blouse, and he shoved her roughly to the ground.

'I'm out of wire,' he said, walking to the side of the barn. 'This here rope'll do.'

He picked up a length of it and returned to Marigold, who was getting to her feet. Then he punched her in the face.

'Strip and lie down next to Joyce,' he said.

But Marigold didn't move. So he picked her up like a side of beef and threw her down in the pool of blood.

'Strip,' he said, 'or I'll cut your snatch.'

Marigold pulled her clothes off and lay down. Then he tied her to her dead sister by the ankle.

'That'll make it harder for you to run away,' he said. 'I think I'll have me some dessert now, then Shepherd, you're gonna fuck Marigold.'

He went over to Holly and untied her. She got up and tried to run, but he grabbed her and ripped off her blouse. He had her on the ground as he cut her dress from her, then he sliced her underwear from her skin.

'Unfriendly end or friendly end,' he said. 'Let's see.'

Temple Jones put the blade inside Holly, and she began to scream. The noise pierced my ears and blocked out all other sound completely as he cut her womanhood apart.

He stopped and raised his head.

Then I heard sirens. Temple Jones ran outside. I waited, watching Holly stagger to her feet, blood streaming down her legs. She went over to Marigold, and they both began to sob. The sirens were getting louder now. I heard cars drawing up in the snow. There was the sound of footsteps, and two police officers came in.

They had their guns raised, and they checked the barn, going behind the stacked wood at the back. Then they untied us and helped us outside.

19.

Temple Jones got away.

Officers searched the nearby woods while we were taken to hospital. Holly was kept in overnight. She'd lost a lot of blood. My head was stitched while Marigold was seen by a doctor. I told the police that Temple Jones may have gone to my house. When I called Mary on my cell phone Tom was still there. Her voice was strained with anxiety.

'Shepherd, what's happened?' she said.

'Temple Jones was here.'

'My God.'

'He's killed Joyce.'

'Dear God.'

'I think he'd have killed us all.'

'Tom called the police and had them go out to Holly's place when you didn't return. Have they got him?'

'He fled the scene. Tell Tom to lock the doors and wait until I get back.'

I gave my statement to the police and explained that Temple Jones and Maxwell Heed were the same person. Two police officers drove Marigold and me back to her house where I helped her pack some things. Then one of the officers drove her back with me, while his colleague followed in my pickup.

All the way there I kept thinking about why Temple Jones had targeted us. That night a manhunt was launched.

Mary put Marigold to bed when we got home. We gave her Felton's old room. After Tom left I sat in the kitchen with Mary and told her about the events in the barn, measuring the effect of my words carefully.

'If we'd never let Maxwell stay, this wouldn't have happened,' she said. 'He's faceless. I keep seeing him, that deformity holding a knife, whispering obscenely in my ear.'

'He was wearing a mask, Mary, that was what you saw when he attacked you. He had it on while he held us prisoner. And he removed it. Temple Jones is Maxwell.'

'What do you mean?'

'Maxwell Heed doesn't exist. He is Temple Jones.'

20.

The manhunt involved the entire Vermont police force. They searched the woods, made random stops on cars leaving the state, checked disused buildings in the area, and printed a police sketch of Temple Jones. Their hunt wasn't helped by the fact that snow had begun to fall again. They didn't find him.

Some days later a hitchhiker said he'd seen a pickup leave some woods and get onto a road a few miles away from Holly's house. He'd tried to hitch a ride and got a good look at the driver. When shown the police sketch he said that was the man. The police searched the woods near the road. They found a disused barn with its doors open and tire marks inside it. It seems Temple Jones left the state before the hunt got underway.

I waited for him, expecting him to return, but he didn't. And I watched the women in my family live in their wounds. When Holly left hospital she came to live with us. She stayed in the spare room. I wandered the house at night with my shotgun. I existed in the self-searing rage of the impotent.

* * *

We buried Joyce a few weeks later. It was only us there; it seemed fitting that the people who'd suffered at the hands of Temple Jones were the ones who said good-bye to her. There was a moment as they lowered the coffin into the frozen ground when the wind dropped. The air felt like ice, and I thought I saw him moving beyond the graves, a spectral presence watching us.

I read the newspapers daily looking for a mention of something that might give me a clue as to where he was. But nothing appeared, and the months passed and the snow began to melt. I spoke to the police, who informed me he was nowhere to be found in Vermont. The New Hampshire police were also on the lookout for him, but there had been no sightings. Everything he said may have been a lie, he could have been anywhere. The hunt for him faded away.

Holly became watchful of Marigold. And religious.It was something I didn't enjoy seeing since it reminded me of Temple Jones's deception. My sister had never shown an interest in the Bible before. Then one day I heard an argument between her and Marigold. They were in the spare room.

'I don't want it,' Marigold said.

'It is the only way you can get through this.'

'Why should I have it?'

'Have the child or you will be a killer like him.'

They came into the kitchen a few minutes later. Mary was wiping dishes, and I was pouring coffee.

'Holly, what was the finding by the doctor when Marigold was examined?' I said.

'The finding?'

'Did they check for pregnancy?'

'Mom, you may as well tell him,' Marigold said.

'She's having the baby.'

'Do you know what you're saying? You're asking her to have Temple Jones's child,' I said.

'She's not going to be a murderer like him.'

'What do you want, Marigold?' Mary said.

'We'll bring it up together,' Holly said.

'Mom, you saw what he did to me. I don't want it.'

'We can call her Joyce if it's a girl.'

'Holly,' I said, but my sister was far away with something inside her that I didn't recognise.

21.

The pregnancy changed Marigold. She would sit alone in the darkness of Felton's room rocking on her heels, staring out of the window at a blackened landscape. She avoided eye contact and never talked about her pregnancy. Her friends' attempts to make contact with her went unacknowledged, as if reminders of her past were unwelcome. She attempted to hide the change in her body, calling her belly 'a distortion.' She took to wearing shapeless baggy clothes and pacing the house at night, moaning, 'I will be slim tomorrow, the nightmare is almost at an end, Joyce let's go to the barn together, he was never there.' I used to hear her stand at the foot of the stairs saying this over and over like a mantra in a mental hospital. The tension in our house was impossible to bear at times. I nursed the consoling idea that I would take afternoons away from the three wounded women and walk in the forest as I used to. But it was where I found him and I never went. It was as if he was still waiting for me out there, readying himself to finish us all off.

Marigold stopped going to university immediately after that day in the barn. It was clear to me and Mary that her mental state was declining by the day. She argued with Holly about the pregnancy and what it entailed, saying there would be no child. She would sleep holding the blouse Joyce had worn the day before she was killed, as if her sister was the last tie to a past that no longer existed for her. And she talked to Joyce alone in her room. I could hear her telling Joyce about the day as twilight fell beyond the aching window panes.

She and Holly continued to live with us, in our wounded home. Their house remained unoccupied. The women circled one another like beggars at times, each needing something no one could give to them. I sat and pondered what it was, and realised one evening that we all wanted ourselves back. We'd lost recognition of who we were. Temple Jones had tied us to his hatred and corrupted our bodies and our minds, as effectively as if he'd forced us to engage in his own acts of defilement and butchery.

During those tortured months of gestation I tried talking to Holly about the pregnancy. I tried to persuade her to let Marigold abort it, but she became angry and unreasonable. Mary tried too but was met with the same response. I watched Marigold withdraw into a troubled world, isolated, fearful of motherhood. The future I'd seen for her had been obliterated by Temple Jones. He dwelt in our house as a shadow. I used to wake at night and stare out of the window believing he was out there.

Marigold said something one day shortly before she went into labour. We were having lunch at the kitchen table. Mary had made a salad, and we were eating cold cuts of meat.

'Carrying this child has changed me,' Marigold said.

'You see, I was right to make you bear it,' Holly said.

'It hasn't changed me in the way you think.'

'You'll see when she's born.'

'I think I've learned to hate now; every time his offspring kicks inside me, it's as though he's raping me again.'

'Don't you dare talk like that,' Holly said, 'you still have your womanhood.'

'You're not carrying his child.'

'If I had more than this lump of butcher's meat between my legs that he left me with I would, I would give anything to bring life into this situation.'

'Temple Jones brings only genital misery.'

'He didn't cut you between the legs.'

'It's prolonging what he did to me. When the baby comes out of me it will feel like his knife again, raping me from the inside. He's invaded my womanhood and stolen my mind.'

'You will bring this baby up; it will be a child of God.'

'What is there that is godly about Temple Jones?'

'We will follow the Bible.'

'I hope I lose it.'

Holly stood up and slapped Marigold across the face. She left the table, and Marigold sat there with a bright red mark burning on her cheek.

I'd never heard them talk to each other like this. I looked away and saw Temple Jones feeding Mary with some of her own salad as he raped her with the handle of the knife. He lived with us, his violations dwelling like a parasite inside us.

After we'd cleared the table, Holly re-entered the kitchen. She walked over to Marigold.

'By having the child you will forgive, it will cleanse you of the anger,' she said.

I thought of what Temple Jones had said when he pretended to be Maxwell and talked of forgiving the man who'd murdered Anna Belle. But there was no Anna Belle and there was no Maxwell and Holly's words seemed formed of the same lies that entire episode of Temple Jones's stay with us was.

I feared for the child's future. Holly asked me to drive her to her house one day. She returned with some of Joyce's old baby clothes. She folded them obsessively and laid them in neat piles on her bed, making sure they sat side by side in a symmetrical pattern. She caressed them, her eyes wandering. Then Marigold screamed, and her waters broke. We rushed her to the hospital as Holly told her she had the baby's clothes ready.

But it wasn't a girl. It was a boy that Marigold gave birth to, and they named him Justin.

22.

Marigold went into labour prematurely. The baby was born at six months. I was there when Holly went in to look at him. Marigold was lying in the hospital bed, her head turned away, and Holly picked the baby up. She'd brought some of Joyce's clothes. She looked at him for a long time.

'These will fit perfectly,' she said.

'He's a boy, Mom,' Marigold said, without looking at her.

'He can wear her clothes.'

'They said they're keeping him here for a while.'

They kept him in observation for days. The fact that he was premature brought with it difficulties, although the extent of them would not be seen for some years.

* * *

They lived with us for the first year of Justin's life. Holly became more emphatic in her religion. She also took charge of Justin's upbringing. She insisted on making him wear Joyce's clothes, and people thought the baby was a girl, something that Holly made no effort to correct. She argued with Marigold for hours about the importance of breastfeeding him, but Marigold refused, and so Holly bottle-fed him.

Marigold withdrew from motherhood. She didn't pick

Justin up but used to sit and watch her mother with him, resentment in her eyes. She stayed at our house, rarely venturing outside, never seeing her friends. I suggested counselling for both of them, but Holly refused.

'The Bible is all we need,' she said.

Marigold became more isolated in her pain, while Holly became a mother again, but she treated Justin like a girl. She talked to him, but what she said were a series of moral statements and commands, and I felt as though she were trying to steal any trace of masculinity he may have. Justin lived in Holly's utterances and denial like an asexual silkworm drowning in poisoned milk. Marigold and Holly existed apart from me and Mary, locked inside Temple Jones's legacy.

Eventually they moved back to their house. I left them there one afternoon the following summer. As I drove away I looked at the barn, and its wood seemed blood red now, a wounded building on an altered landscape. I told myself that we would once again picnic outside it in a summer when the injuries had faded from our memories, and I realised I was tired of lying. I returned home and drank some whisky and walked about the house, just me and Mary now, lost in our grief. But what it was we were grieving was more than the loss of Felton, it was the loss of our sense that the world was to be trusted. I stared at the landscape, summoning from it the reassurance it had always held. I felt a spark of my old feelings as I looked at the mountains in the distance, then I saw Temple Jones standing at the top of one of them with his spurs digging into the earth and a smirk on his face.

I visited Marigold and Holly every day. It was as if I was trying to reclaim part of the old life, the one that Temple Jones broke. But I knew I secretly feared some catastrophe, as if Holly could not be trusted with the care of a child. She took charge more and more of Justin's upbringing while Marigold retreated further from the world. Holly made up her mind that they would live there alone and she would school Justin herself. And I wondered if Temple Jones would return.

23.

Then one day I read something in the newspapers. Two black teenagers had been assaulted in Massachusetts. Their abductor had tied them up in a garage and raped both of them with various objects before murdering one of them. He'd beaten the other one badly, and she was in the hospital. I knew it was him.

A man like Temple Jones has to rape and defile. It's like food to him. I knew when he disappeared he would commit more attacks, but this was the first time I'd read of one that had his signature. The police had no information on the attacker and were waiting to interview the sister who'd survived. I showed the article to Mary.

'It's him,' I said.

'It looks like it.'

'Should I warn Holly?'

'Do you think she'll listen?'

'They're living alone, how would they defend themselves against a second attack by him?'

'Why would he risk coming back?'

'He's a few hours drive away.'

'What would he have to gain?'

'He didn't finish what he was trying to do that day.'

I waited to get more information before talking to Holly.

A few days later the police interviewed the sister. As she described her attacker, she described Temple Jones. The things he'd done, the things he said were too similar to what he did to Marigold and Joyce that day for it not to be Temple Jones. This time there were no other people involved.

I wondered where he would go to now. Another manhunt was launched as the police made the connection between the two cases. I told Holly and asked her and Marigold to come and live with us. She refused. I told her my concern that Temple Jones would come back again.

'Then I will deal with him,' she said.

'At least let me leave you with a gun.'

She did. I bought her a Remington shotgun. I followed the manhunt. Once again they didn't catch him.

I spoke to the police and got a good account of what Temple Jones had done. The sister he'd attacked said she hadn't seen him before and didn't know his name. The things he said to her and her sister made her believe he'd been watching them.

He'd described the journey they took on their way home from work. He'd raped both sisters with a screwdriver. He'd tortured them for hours. But there was one thing he said that turned my blood to ice. After he killed one sister, he said to the surviving one, 'You're a messenger now; tell all the pure of heart I'm coming. I want certain people to know what I'm doing and they know who they are and the corruptions they're hiding, for they're the ones I hate the most, all those morally pure men and women who are stained worse than a whorehouse bed.'

24.

I watched Justin grow, unsure of who his mother was and ignored by Marigold. And I became more and more concerned for her mental state and Holly's. My sister sank deeper into a form of religion that denied the person I knew her to be. Temple Jones's actions had denied her access to who she was. I struggled to overcome my sense of alienation, but there was no reaching her. Each attempt I made to get her to see what was happening was rebuffed.

Marigold became more and more mentally ill. She rarely spoke and walked about the house staring into the distance.

There were no further articles in the newspapers about the man who'd attacked the black teenagers. There were no further attacks that I read of.

And I thought about him, Temple Jones. I spoke to Mary of my concerns.

'I think he wants to return and kill us all.'

'Even at the risk of his own capture?'

'If he can get away with it.'

'I just want to forget about him; he stands between me and my grief for Felton like a stone bruise in my soul.'

But there would be no forgetting Temple Jones. He lived on in the pain he inflicted. He had violated the women in my family in so many ways he'd left me with people I struggled to relate to. He fed on purity; his hunger to corrupt both savage and sexual, he found pleasure in inflicting pain.

I thought of the split man that Temple Jones was and the fiction that was Maxwell Heed. I thought of how he'd made himself beyond suspicion.

25.

He did return, as I knew he would. I heard the rowels of his spurs clicking on the ground outside the back door before I saw him. The noise sounded like someone spinning the chamber of a gun. He was sitting on the well in the bright sunlight. He dug his heels into the ground.

He saw me looking at him through the kitchen window. He moved his boots, and I heard the clink of his spurs against the sandstone.

I picked up the phone, but the line had been cut. My cell phone was upstairs, and I didn't want to risk going up to get it. And so I went to get my Winchester from the living room. When I came back into the kitchen, I was about to call out to Mary when I felt a hand on my shoulder. I turned round, and Temple Jones punched me in the face, knocking me to the ground.

When I got up he was holding my gun. Mary was coming downstairs. I could see her in the hallway. She looked into the kitchen and froze. Temple Jones reached into his pocket and removed some rope.

'Mary, you can tie him up,' he said, 'or I'll rape you and Marigold.'

'You'll probably do that anyway.'

'OK, then I'll get the knife, and I'll use the other end on you this time. I'll cut you so bad you won't be able to pee.'

She came into the room. I sat in a chair while Mary tied my hands behind my back.

'And his legs,' Temple Jones said.

'What are you going to do? The entire Vermont police force is looking for you,' I said.

'Mary, sit down.'

He tied her into a chair. Then he inspected my ropes and tightened them.

He walked across the room, his rowels loud on the wooden floor. He stood so we could both see him, his back to the wall, away from the window.

'Who do you think I am?' he said.

'A man who needs to defile, who must feel so corrupt he hates the idea of purity,' I said.

'You believe in purity, do you Shepherd?'

'I believe it's something you've never experienced.'

'I've experienced it all right, or the pretence of it in all the young whores I've screwed.'

'You're a sick man,' Mary said.

'You think I'm sick of snatch? Maybe I'll have a taste of yours before I leave. I remember you were still tight for a woman of your age. Will you moan for me, Mary? Remember the noise you made that day? I saw it in your eyes, the enjoyment you got when I put the handle inside you. Shepherd wasn't here, and you let loose a lot of your raw sexuality. I can think of things I could do that would stir you up further.'

'You think the sound a person makes when they're in pain is pleasure,' Mary said.

I let him talk and tried to undo the knots on my wrists.

'Now those nieces of yours tasted good, Shepherd. How

is young Marigold?'

'She'll never be the same.'

'That right?'

'It is. You've destroyed lives for no reason.'

'Did you read about the two black girls?'

'I knew that was you.'

'And I knew you'd read about it.'

'I put you up. I invited you into my home, and you violated my wife and nieces and killed Joyce. You butchered my sister, and you killed Owen.'

'And you still to this day don't know why. I knew you'd find me in that forest. You took that walk regularly, Shepherd. I waited for you.'

'Why didn't you just break in and attack us?'

'I imagine that question has been playing on your mind.'

'That wouldn't have given you as much pleasure, would it?' Mary said.

'You think Shepherd is a pure man?'

'He's a good man who gave you shelter.'

'Well let me tell you a story. There was a woman who met a man many years ago in New Hampshire. This man lived in rural Vermont and was attracted to her. He slept with her a few times on business trips, having met her through his business. But her sexual desires troubled him, she was somewhat wild in bed, and he left her. The woman had a boy. She continued to indulge her sexual predilections, exposing the boy to certain sights a child simply shouldn't see or he may grow up with strange cravings.'

'Where is all this going?' Mary said.

'Where do you think it's going, Shepherd?'

'No doubt this is your account of your childhood, and you blame your behaviour on that,' Mary said.

'The woman's name was Francine Rothwell, and she was a good-looking woman. She married a man called Samuel Jones. The boy's name was Maxwell, and Samuel Jones beat and abused him. The boy was born about twenty-seven years ago, a year or so after Felton was born. Does the name Francine Rothwell mean anything to you, Shepherd?'

As he was talking I froze. I could feel Mary's eyes on my face.

'I remember.'

'Shepherd, what is this about?' Mary said.

'I had a brief affair with her.'

'You ain't so pure after all,' Temple Jones said. 'My real name is Maxwell Temple Heed Jones. I am your son, and I killed Felton.

26.

It was many years since I'd thought about Francine Rothwell. My affair with her had been brief, and I ended it because I was disturbed by her behaviour.

It happened early in my marriage to Mary. I was running a small hardware business at the time and used to visit neighbouring states to discuss orders other stores wanted to make from my catalogue. Francine worked for a hardware store in New Hampshire, just outside Lebanon. She was young, attractive, and overtly sexual. We had many meetings before I slept with her. It happened one weekend when I was feeling alone and had drunk too much.

I regretted it from the first time and hid my guilt from Mary. But while Francine was sexually appealing she also began to make demands in bed I found disconcerting. She wanted to be tied up. She wanted to be treated roughly, and I refused, which made her angry. I never considered that she might have become pregnant.

At that time Mary was heavily engaged in looking after Felton, who was only a few months old. I thought about why I'd strayed and concluded I was feeling left out.

I never had any other affairs, nor was I tempted to. I isolated the incident in my mind as an anomaly that lay at the beginning of my marriage. As I was faced with Temple Jones's revelation my guilt flooded back. Mary knew now, and she knew I'd kept this from her all these years. But another part of my mind questioned the truth of what Temple Jones was saying. He claimed to be my son, but how did I know this was true? And I thought how the darkness I'd seen in his mother in bed was alive in him.

'How do you know Shepherd is your father?' Mary said.

'My mother claimed it all along. She never deviated from the story. And besides, while I lived here I took some of Shepherd's hair from his comb and sent a sample of it together with some of mine to a private lab that can verify paternity. The results proved he is my father.'

'Is that why you lived with us? To find that out?' Mary said.

'That was part of it, but I also wanted to meet the family.'

'You mean rape my nieces?' I said.

'What's yours is mine, huh?'

'No, what's mine is not yours. You were a mistake, Temple; that is all.'

'I remember that October morning. I'd been watching Felton for some time, handsome young man he was. Mary didn't like him using guns, so he shot deer with a bow and arrow. I'm a good shot myself. I was some feet above him behind a tree when I let that arrow fly. It pierced his throat.'

'You can't destroy us with your revelation,' Mary said.

There was no recrimination towards me from her, but I sensed she didn't want Temple Jones to feel he had the upper hand and so she wouldn't show it in front of him.

'My childhood was a sorry affair. My mother enjoyed bringing men back to the house and using ropes and various other ties. I saw her at it; perhaps that's why I enjoy doing the things I do. But then again I know that the teenagers I've enjoyed derived great pleasure from the acts; it's simply their beliefs that prevented them from admitting to it.'

'No woman enjoys being raped,' Mary said.

'We might put that to the test in a little while. I think I'll just hitch up your skirt and feel my way inside you with something hard and see if you moan again. Shepherd never had the satisfaction of hearing the sounds you made last time. I do believe you were about to ask me to do something else to you. I never got the time, but don't be shy.'

'You expect to get away with this?' I said.

'I believe I do, Shepherd, they ain't caught me yet.'

'They will.'

'You think? I killed your boy, and you never knew it. You thought it was a hunting accident.'

'They'll catch you for your other crimes.'

'I never did finish telling you about my childhood. Eventually my mother married Samuel Jones; he continued my upbringing by beating me with his fists. He also beat my mother. She finally killed him with the broken end of a beer bottle. She cut his throat. She went to jail, and I ain't never seen her again.'

'Do you really think we care?' Mary said.

'No I don't, but I'll make you.'

He walked over to her, the rowels of his spurs scraping the floor. I was still trying to free my hands and felt the rope go slack, but it was not enough for me to pull them out.

Temple Jones lifted Mary's skirt and put his hand between her legs. He pulled a Luger from his belt and began to stroke her leg with it. Then he pushed it between her thighs.

'I think you're going to enjoy this, Mary,' he said. 'I know you don't approve of guns, but imagine it inside you, all that power in your snatch.'

Just then I heard the front door open. Tom had been in the habit of visiting us, and I saw him enter the hallway.

Temple Jones turned with his gun as Tom pulled out his Colt .45. He aimed it at Temple Jones's head.

'Put it down or I'll shoot.'

'Will you?' Temple Jones said, walking towards him.

27.

Just then two things happened. I got my hands loose and managed to stand up, and Tom fired at Temple Jones. He hit him in the shoulder, and Temple Jones fell backwards onto my path as I moved towards him. I grabbed him and tried to strangle him, but he was too strong, my feet were still tied, and I lost my balance. Then he shot Tom.

'I'm gonna come back for you,' Temple Jones said.

He whipped me across the head with his pistol.

* * *

When I came to I could see Tom's feet. I was lying on the floor, and my head throbbed. I got up and untied Mary. Tom wasn't moving, the bullet had hit him in the chest. I called an ambulance, then the police. I'd been unconscious for half an hour. I told the police to go to my sister's house.

The ambulance arrived quickly. I'd bandaged my head by the time they arrived, and Mary went to the hospital.

I picked my Winchester up off the floor and drove to Holly's. When I got there I saw two police cars, but the bodies of the officers lay slumped inside. One of the cars had a shattered windscreen. There was blood on the dash and the seats. The other car had both doors open. The insides of the doors were flecked with blood.

I walked towards the house with my shotgun in front of

me. I opened the front door slowly and went inside.

I will never forget what I saw next. The door to Marigold's bedroom was open, and she was naked and on her hands and knees. Temple Jones was astride her back, digging his spurs into her sides. Marigold was trying to crawl towards the door. Temple Jones had stuck her bra in her mouth and was pulling on the straps as if they were reins. The humiliation and despair in her eyes took me back to that day in the barn when he killed Joyce. I looked at the blood on his shoulder and aimed my shotgun at his head.

But just then Holly appeared behind him. Her bedroom adjoined Marigold's, and she was standing at the open door. Her feet were tied, and she was walking slowly and with difficulty.

I was trying to steady my aim on Temple Jones's head as Marigold continued to crawl across the floor. He looked up and saw me.

'You squeeze that trigger, and I'll shoot her dead,' he said, pulling his gun from his belt. 'And I'm a good with a gun, not like Tom, that was a glancing shot, nothing more than a flesh wound.'

'You're not going to shoot anyone,' Holly said.

She had a knife her hand, and as he looked round she stabbed him in the chest. She kept stabbing him until he fell off Marigold, dropping his gun. I heard the noise of Justin's voice behind me. He was walking towards us. Temple Jones was staring at him.

'You didn't know you had a son,' I said.

'Just like you, Shepherd.'

'Well, it's a good thing you'll never have a hand in his upbringing.'

'You mean like the way Dwight Fisher did with me?'

28.

I leaned down and stared into his jade-like eyes.

'Say that again about Dwight Fisher,' I said.

'I lured you into a trap, a series of inventions to mirror your lies.'

'How do you know about him?'

'He brought me up. He hates you, Shepherd. If you ever want a lesson in how to turn a boy into a killer, talk to him.'

'How can I when he disappeared years ago?'

'Go to the square in Lebanon where you met her. You remember Court Street? Just round the corner is a barbershop. He's not hard to find.'

Holly had frozen at the mention of Dwight Fisher's name. She was standing there wringing her hands, staring down at Temple Jones who was fading fast.

'How do you know him?' she said.

'He and Francine Rothwell got hitched.'

'Who's Francine Rothwell?'

'You better ask Shepherd that. He said you used to enjoy it.'

'This is something you've heard somewhere, another one of your lies,' I said.

'Didn't Mary ever tell you?'

'Tell me what?' I said.

But he closed his eyes and coughed blood onto the floor.

29.

Maxwell Temple Heed Jones was wanted for a number of attacks on young women across two states. He'd been preying on them for years. But the thing that baffled everyone was how he'd managed to escape detection for so long. I surmised that he had lived rough and managed to hide out between the attacks, returning when the search for him had ended.

* * *

I couldn't get his words out of my head. I felt flayed, as if I was missing a layer of skin, and I wanted to force his mouth open and make him speak. But Temple Jones was dead, and Holly was arrested and released on bail that I paid.

I told Mary what had happened. I told her what he'd said. She looked away, past the grieving window pane that had become her vista on the world. We were in the kitchen as I asked her the question that unlocked the past.

'Do you feel betrayed by me?' I said.

'We have to put the past behind us.'

'It happened many years ago, and I regretted it ever since. But I kept it hidden from you, and you've only just found out.'

'Sometimes these things happen.'

'You're going to let go of it as easily as that?'

'After what he's done it seems insignificant, and I feel numb.'

'When we let the fiction that was Maxwell Heed into our house, how could we not have sensed what this man was capable of?'

'Shepherd Butler, sometimes you just can't know a man; some men keep things too well hidden.'

'And what about some women, do you think they hide things?'

'People hide things for different reasons. Sometimes it's because they don't want to hurt other people.'

'What did he mean when he said, "Didn't Mary ever tell you?"'

'I accept what you did, Shepherd.'

'Why?'

'Because I refuse to let that man destroy our marriage.'

'I'm going to Lebanon. I'm going to see if Dwight Fisher's still alive.'

'He's still misleading you.'

'Is he?'

30.

It was as I was leaving the next day that she told me. I'd decided that the only way I could determine what had motivated Temple Jones was to see if what he said about Dwight Fisher was true. If he was lying, I couldn't work out how he'd heard of him, especially because Holly never spoke of him and neither did I. I'd decided to drive to Lebanon and spend the day trying to ascertain if anyone had heard of Dwight Fisher. I needed to put Temple Jones to rest. I was standing in the hallway putting on my coat when Mary came out of the kitchen and put her hand on my shoulder.

'You're a good man,' she said.

'It should never have happened.'

I followed her into the kitchen where she sat at the table with tears rolling down her face.

'I didn't tell you for the same reason you didn't tell me,' she said.

'So he knew something. Temple Jones knew more about my affairs than I did.'

'Affairs, yes. Not just yours, Shepherd, he knew.'

'What are you saying?'

'I had an affair with Dwight Fisher.'

I felt an overwhelming sense of vertigo, and Mary suddenly seemed far away.

'How long ago?'

She knew what lay behind my question.

'I'm sorry. Long enough.'

'For what?'

'For it to happen.'

'For what to happen?'

'It was twenty-eight years ago. Long enough for Felton to be conceived.'

I felt winded and sat heavily on a chair.

'You're saying that Felton was Dwight Fisher's son?'

'I'm sorry.'

'How can you be sure?'

'You were away on a business trip when I fell pregnant. It had to be him. You'd been distant with me, and we hadn't made love for some time.'

I remembered the time. It was when I was having the affair with Francine Rothwell, and my guilt had made me distant with Mary.

'Does Holly know?'

'No.'

'I need to find him. I've lost two sons, and both of them were lies.'

'You see, none of us are pure.'

'Is that why Dwight Fisher ran away the first time?'

'Do you remember when your hardware store was burgled?'

'Of course.'

'You'd given Dwight work.'

'He was gambling. Holly was desperate.'

'You've always been charitable, Shepherd, that's one of

the reasons I love you.'

'Did he know you were pregnant?'

'Yes. And I knew he burgled your store. You see, he hadn't stopped gambling. He used the cash to pay off his debts. I'd begun to show, and so I told him if he didn't leave I'd get the law on him. I said I regretted the affair, and I wanted you to bring up the child.'

'The child of another man.'

'You were a wonderful father. I never loved Dwight Fisher.'

'He was my brother-in-law.'

'And he was a womaniser; I wasn't the only one.'

'But he knew you were carrying his child.'

'I wanted it to be yours. He'd begun to frighten me in bed. Behind his looks and charm there was something else. Something I saw in Temple Jones.'

31.

I visited Holly before I left. I sat in her kitchen and asked her about Dwight Fisher. Marigold was sleeping, a habit she'd adopted to avoid the day. Justin was in his room.

'I'm going to Lebanon,' I said. 'I need to find out if he was telling the truth.'

'He can't be, Shepherd.'

'I've never asked you about your marriage. You've never spoken about it.'

'Some things are best not spoken of.'

'Did he mistreat you?'

'Yes.'

'What did he do? I know about the gambling.'

'It was more than that.'

'He was a womaniser.'

'Shepherd, I don't want to talk about it.'

'If he is in any way behind what has happened, I need to know what kind of man I'm dealing with.'

'Dwight Fisher needed to degrade women in bed.'

'Did he rape you?'

'He wanted me to act things out, things I wouldn't do.'

Suddenly Holly wasn't looking at me anymore, but at the past. I felt like an intruder, and so I left.

<h1 style="text-align:center">32.</h1>

I drove there that morning, leaving the mountain road whose familiar beauty now felt like a scar. As I left Stowe, I thought of Dwight Fisher, the missing father, the womaniser, the thief, the gambler, the sexual monster who'd slept with my wife, and I thought of Dwight Fisher the father of my son.

* * *

Court Street formed part of an attractive New England square with a common at its centre. I parked and asked a man who was walking his dog where the barbershop was. He gave me directions, and I found it within minutes. But as I stood outside I wondered how it could lead me to him and the answers I needed, and I began to feel foolish. Was this the last of Temple Jones's lies and had I travelled there on a pointless errand? I decided on a straightforward approach, and I entered the shop.

A large man in a T-shirt I took to be the owner was sweeping the floor.

'You looking for a cut?' he said, glancing over at me.

'No, I'm looking for someone.'

'And who might that be?'

'Dwight Fisher.'

'He's upstairs.'

'How do I get up there?'

'He lives in the apartment. Ring the bell outside.'

'Thank you.'

I didn't expect it to be so simple. Then I realised Temple Jones wanted me to find him. If that was the case he wanted me to find something out. I prepared myself for an unpleasant discovery. I stood in the street and looked at the single bell that sat in the wall to the right of the shop. It bore no name or number but had to be for the apartment. And so I rang it. As I stood there I realised I hadn't prepared what I would say to Dwight Fisher, and I knew that any such preparation was pointless, given how little I'd known about my own family.

I heard the sound of a chain being rattled, then the door opened. A young woman in a blouse and a pair of white shorts stood there looking at me quizzically. Her blouse was only buttoned halfway, and a black bra showed in the gap.

'Is Dwight Fisher there?' I said.

'Upstairs.'

She jerked her head in the direction of a staircase at the end of the grimy corridor and stood there looking at me as if I were a misfit.

'Is it OK if I go up?' I said.

'I reckon he's done with me.'

She slipped on a pair of bright red shoes that she picked up from behind the door, raising her eyes to my face as she bent. Then she walked out into the street leaving me standing in front of the open door thinking about the words she'd used.

I walked in, closing the door behind me, and climbed the staircase. There was a door at the top, and I knocked.

Hearing no noise from inside, I turned the handle cautiously and walked in. The apartment had a small corridor with several doors off it. To my right I could see a living room, and I walked into it and stared at the sofa, TV set, chairs, and faded carpet. Then I saw him. He was in the corridor tucking his shirt into his faded jeans. He looked up and stared at me, and I knew he knew me. His shirt was pearl-coloured, and black hair showed obscenely on his muscular chest as he tucked it into his jeans, sliding it down past the black leather belt, which had a silver buckle that displayed a naked cowgirl reclining in only her hat and boots. He picked up a bottle of Jack Daniels from a table and walked into the living room.

'To what do I owe this pleasure, Shepherd?' he said.

'Temple Jones.'

33.

He swigged from the bottle and wiped his mouth with the back of his hand. He was as I remembered him, relatively unchanged, but older, and bearing a look of degeneracy in his face. He was still a handsome man, with deep blue eyes, a good complexion, and thick hair the colour of platinum that he wore swept back on his forehead. He picked up a packet of Marlboros from the coffee table, pulled a Zippo lighter from his pocket, lit the cigarette, and took a deep drag, all the while keeping his gaze locked on me.

'What's he done now?' he said.

'Far too much, but he won't be doing it anymore.'

'Can I pour you a shot?'

'I haven't come here to drink.'

'It's been a long time, Shepherd.'

'It was over twenty-eight years ago.'

'Was it?'

'That you had an affair with my wife.'

He took another drink of Jack Daniels, narrowing his eyes at me.

'That what she tell you?' he said.

'It's what I know to be true.'

'I don't reckon you've come all the way here to talk about that.'

'Don't you?'

'How is Mary?'

'Not good, not good at all.'

'So what's this about Temple Jones?'

'He lived in my house for a while, disguised as someone else. He called himself Maxwell Heed, then he raped Mary with the handle of a knife, raped my nieces and killed one of them, and butchered my sister.'

'That boy was never any good. His real name's Maxwell Heed. He renamed himself Temple Jones after he got a taste for hookers, and he had quite a taste I can tell you.'

He spat a piece of tobacco off his tongue.

'Holly will never recover. You do remember Holly, you were married to her?'

'Sounds like you're real bitter with me,' he said.

'Wouldn't you be?'

'Over the affair?'

'I only just found out.'

'Well, well, Mary was a better liar than I thought she'd be.'

'You haven't even asked about your daughters.'

'Who did he kill?'

'Joyce.'

'And how is Marigold?'

'Depressed, broken.'

'If I catch up with him I'll take my belt to him.'

'He's dead; Holly killed him.'

'No shit?'

'And he told me to come and speak to you.'

34.

He stubbed his cigarette out in an ashtray.

'Speak to me about what?'

'He said you brought him up.'

'I tried. But with a boy like that there's not much you can do.'

'He said you and Francine Rothwell got hitched.'

'Did he?'

'Is it true?'

'That boy sure did some talking.'

'Is she his mother?'

'In a manner of speaking.'

'Dwight I want answers, I know about the burglary.'

'What do you wanna know?'

'Why Temple Jones came looking for me, why he raped your daughters, killed Joyce, mutilated Holly, and violated my wife.'

'He had it in him.'

'Had what in him?'

'Tendencies towards extreme acts.'

'He said he was brought up by a man called Samuel Jones.'

'Bullshit.'

'He said Samuel Jones beat and abused him, and that his mother brought men back to the house and he witnessed certain events, events of a sexual nature. According to Temple Jones, she killed Samuel Jones with a beer bottle and went to jail.'

'I never heard such a load of shit in my life.'

'So what's the truth?'

'He was brought up real well, had a good life. He went to Dartmouth College in Hanover, well educated, he was an Ivy League boy, but he had some rather strange appetites.'

'He said he was a chef.'

'Learned it in the army.'

'He said I'm his father.'

'No, that can't be, that can't be at all.'

35.

'Why do you say that?' I said.

'There's only one man who could be that boy's father.'

'You seem pretty sure. And why is that?'

'Because there was only one man who was sleeping with his mother at the time he was conceived.'

'And who was that?'

'You're looking at him, Shepherd.'

'Who is his mother?'

'Francine.'

It all made sense. Dwight accompanied me on a couple of business trips. As I stood there in his living room I had a recollection of the night when he must have discovered I was having an affair with Francine. We were staying in a hotel, and I had booked a room for her, since she lived some distance away from the meetings we were having with local businesses. I left Francine's room late that night and thought I heard a door close in the corridor as I did. It sounded like the door to Dwight's room, but as I turned to assess where the sound had come from a woman stepped out of the room directly opposite.

I concluded that she was the source of the noise and returned to my own room where I went to bed and didn't give the matter a second thought. Dwight's behaviour never altered towards me, as an employee he was polite, as a brother-in-law somewhat distant but friendly. He never gave me cause for suspicion that he knew. But he must have known.

There was another incident I remembered as I stood there looking at him. Shortly before I broke off the affair with Francine I thought I saw him flirting with her, and I wondered if he was interested in her. We'd all had dinner at the hotel, and I'd gone to bed early, wanting to avoid Francine as I thought about how to end it. I couldn't sleep and came back down to the bar an hour later for a night cap. Dwight and Francine were still there, seated over in a corner of the bar, and they didn't see me. Dwight was leaning across the small table that stood between them saying something to her, and he touched her arm as she laughed.

I dismissed the incident and decided definitely to end the affair. Her behaviour in bed had become disturbing, and my guilt towards Mary had grown too heavy to bear.

I looked into Dwight's eyes now as he stood there measuring my response.

'When did you start seeing her?' I said.

'Does it matter?'

'Yes it matters.'

'Shortly after I left.'

'Why?'

'She's a good-looking woman.'

'You know about me and her.'

'Of course.'

It all began to piece itself together, like a series of broken bones forming a skeleton. I remembered something Holly said to me shortly after Dwight disappeared for good.

'I think Dwight felt he couldn't live up to you as the man of the family. I think he wanted what you have, Shepherd.'

It was one of the few times she spoke of him.

'Did you tell Mary?' I said to Dwight.

'About your affair with Francine?'

I nodded.

'Mary knows,' he said.

She'd accepted the revelation years ago because of her own guilt and sense that she'd committed a deeper wrong than I had. It occurred to me now that her knowledge that I'd betrayed her motivated her to hide Felton's paternity from me. Or did she not believe Dwight when he told her that I'd been having an affair? Suddenly I was back in the red barn with Temple Jones looking down at me. Since that day my own life had become untrustworthy. Did I know Mary? I had to regain the things I trusted. I needed to taste purity again.

As I looked at Dwight his face was full of sexual depravity. There was laughter in his eyes.

'How did Mary take it when you told her?' I said.

'She was more interested in getting rid of me.'

'And why was that?'

'I think she wanted a stable family life.'

'Or was it because of something you did to her? Something you did in bed?'

'Like what?'

'Before I left to come here I spoke to Holly about you. She said you needed to degrade women. She said you wanted her to act things out in bed. What exactly is it you do?'

'Most women can't live with their own pleasure.'

'What sort of things do you do?' I said, taking a step towards him.

'Nothing they don't enjoy.'

He sounded like Temple Jones; he even looked like him

in that moment.

'You mean you coerce them to engage in things they can't live with?' I said.

'That seems a fancy way of saying I let them find out who they are.'

I thought of Francine and her demands.

'Do you tie them up?' I said.

'Some of them, you'll be amazed at the things women get into. I've seen nice clean college girls behave like hookers, housewives get dirtier than you'd ever imagine.'

'That's why you and Francine got it on, you share the same tastes. I remember what she wanted me to do to her.'

'She'd already been broken in.'

'What sort of things did you want my sister to act out?'

'You want me to tell you what I do in bed?'

'Did you hurt her?'

'A woman often does things that her moral conscience can't let her live with. It's hypocrisy, sex is part of the animal inside us.'

I thought of Temple Jones's words in the red barn as he violated Joyce.

'They "want the rough and ready sex of animals in a field,"' I said.

'I couldn't have put it better myself,' Dwight said.

'Those are your son's words.'

'That right? Do you know that boy stole from me?'

'I'd say he learned from you. I'd say you turned him into the predator that he was.'

'I even covered for him when he got in trouble with that knife of his.'

'What had he done?'

'Frightened some college girl by threatening to stuff the blade inside her.'

'He learned it all from you.'

'Learned what? I don't use knives in the bedroom.'

'I think I'm getting the picture of what you make women do.'

'Oh yeah?'

'Do you ride them?'

'They enjoy the pleasures I introduce them to, why do you think they stick around?'

'Why on earth did my sister ever marry you?'

'Because I made her come, just like I made Mary come.'

'There's no purity in you; you derive pleasure from corruption.'

'Fuck purity.'

That was when I hit him with a blistering roundhouse that knocked him onto the sofa. And I kept on hitting him until he just lay there staring up at me, his face torn and bruised, his lips mashed, his head running with blood. He stared at me with shock and incomprehension, and I pulled myself away and down the stairs and into the street. A woman was standing outside the door, and I recognised her. She'd kept her figure, but as I looked into her small dark eyes I saw stress in her face and a look of entrapment that didn't use to be there.

Francine Rothwell stood there looking up at me. With her dark hair and full mouth she looked much the same.

'Shepherd, what are you doing here?' she said.

'Is there somewhere we can talk?'

36.

There was a café nearby, and we sat at a table at the back. We ordered coffee, and I told her about what Temple Jones had done and the things Holly had said about Dwight.

As I spoke she occasionally looked at me with a pained expression, then looked away, dropping her eyes to the surface of the table. When I finished she sat without saying anything for a while, staring out of the window at the street. She was still an attractive woman. There was a permanent sexual inquisitiveness in her eyes, as if a lifetime's habit of wanting certain things had set its own expression there.

'What Holly said is true,' she said.

'About Dwight.'

'He always wanted what you had, even me. I sometimes think that's why he started the affair with me. He knew about you and me, although I didn't find that out until later. He was obsessed by you for years, blamed you for things.'

'What sort of things?'

'Anything that put him in touch with his own corruption.'

'He hates purity, doesn't he? He feels threatened by it.'

'He does. He hates it, and he's drawn to it. It's the thing he wants most. He's attracted to a certain kind of woman, then he wants to corrupt her. He'll test a woman's purity until she yields to his depravity, to prove her purity was a lie.'

'I'm sure he had no problem with what you like in bed.'

'Oh, Dwight's too extreme for me, some of the things he's into.'

'He doesn't speak highly of his own son.'

'Shepherd, Maxwell never stood a chance.'

37.

'When he stayed with us he used the name Maxwell Heed while he plotted his acts of violence and violation. He said his real name was Maxwell Temple Heed Jones.'

'He was born Maxwell Heed. He renamed himself Temple Jones. Do you want to know why?'

'So Heed is a surname, how come when his father's name is Fisher? Are you saying Dwight isn't his father?'

'Dwight's his father all right, some father he was to Maxwell. He was coming and going all the time. I'll tell you how Maxwell was brought up, with Dwight's fists and belt. That boy was sent home from school black and blue, we were pronounced unfit parents.'

'Why did he hate him so much?'

'I think he reminded him of himself. Maxwell and Dwight are alike. And I think deep down Dwight hates himself, but he chooses to think about hating you. He used to dwell on the fact that you were bringing up his other son.'

'So you know about him and Mary.'

'I know all right. He wanted to bring up that boy. Do you know what she said to him? Do you know what Mary told Dwight when she got rid of him?'

'I believe she threatened to inform the police about the burglary he committed at my store.'

Francine shook her head.

'I ain't never heard of that before, although it don't surprise me he'd rob. No, what Mary said was that he was diseased, sexually, and you were a pure man and it was you she wanted to raise her child.'

'I think it's more than likely the threat of the law got rid of him. I don't think Dwight would care what she thought of him.'

'Maybe, maybe both things got to him, but I know his hatred for Maxwell stemmed from what she said to him.'

'You were telling me why Maxwell renamed himself.'

'It began with the beatings and the things his father said to him. It started young, too. If Maxwell did anything to rile Dwight, he hit him. By the time he was eight years old, Maxwell had been punched. As a teenager, Dwight whipped Maxwell with his belt. And what he used to say was, "You better be good, Maxwell. I got another son, way better than you, a pure boy; you better try to be as good as him." And he brought you into it.'

'What did he say to him about me?'

'"There's a man called Shepherd Butler; he's a morally self-righteous piece of shit. He looks down his nose at the likes of us. He wouldn't even let you in his house. He has a son called Felton, but he's my son. He's the son I wish I had, not you. You better behave, or I'll whip you until you bleed." I can see it now, walking in on him thrashing Maxwell. He used to make him strip, and he'd beat him.'

'Well it's clear to me that the acts Temple Jones perpetrated in the red barn stem from Dwight's treatment of him as a child.'

'It got worse, Shepherd, I used to fear Dwight would kill him. I can't count the number of times he beat him, blaming you, telling him how a man like you wouldn't let him in his home, how his other son was his superior in every way.'

'It's as if he was inciting him to do the things he did.'

'I tried to stop him, but Dwight beat me too, and I had to cope with what he was doing to me in bed and the other women.'

'Why have you stayed with him?'

'There's the other side to him, the sweet side I crave. Dwight is such a handsome man. And when he's not riled up he makes me feel things that give me a real deep down warmth. There are two sides to him.'

'You know, a lot of women stay with violent men because they think it will stop. They put up with the humiliation because of that sweet side you talk about.'

'Don't get me wrong, he doesn't beat me often, not like he did with Maxwell. And there are times I deserved it, like when he found me with other men.'

'But it's OK for him to have other women?'

'They work for him.'

'What are you saying?'

'Dwight's a pimp, but I'm his girl.'

I realised there was no getting through to her; she was hooked to the sexual corruption.

'Dwight claims Temple Jones went to Dartmouth College. He paints an extremely different picture of his childhood than the one Temple Jones did.'

'Maxwell went to Dartmouth College all right, but not as a student, he went there to pick up girls, because he felt if he could get an Ivy League girl he wasn't this inferior piece of shit his father said he was.'

'Dwight said he threatened a student with his knife.'

'That's right, his knife, he called it the thing every woman wants. He did, but only after what his father did.'

'And what was that?'

'How sordid do you want this to get?'

'I want to understand how all of this came about.'

'Maxwell picked up a college student, real pretty she was, and innocent. He brought her home to impress his father, told him he'd met her family and they were real wealthy and how they liked Maxwell. It was all a lie of course. It was his first date, he was fifteen, looked older; the girl was nineteen. You know what Dwight did? He screwed her, sent Maxwell out on an errand and used his charms to get her into bed. Dwight's real good at getting women into bed. When Maxwell came back from the errand he found the door locked. When he was finally let in he saw the girl dressing in our bedroom. She told him he was too young for her. Then Dwight gave Maxwell a blow-by-blow account of what he did to her, describing her tits and her pussy and the sound she made when she came.'

'Is that the girl he threatened?'

'It is. He went to her room and took out his knife. He tried to strip her, but she fought and made a commotion and Maxwell got in trouble.'

'Dwight says he covered for him.'

'He did. He said Maxwell had been with him all day and the girl was making it up, that she'd made a play for Dwight and he'd rejected her, that she was taking it out on Maxwell.'

'Were the police involved?'

'Briefly, then the incident was dropped. Dwight knew one of the officers. He was one of Dwight's customers. Dwight gave him some cash. Dwight has a lot of connected customers.'

'You're talking about prostitution.'

'Yeah, he sells them pleasure, any kind of pleasure they want.'

'He didn't punish Maxwell?'

'He did, but not until later. He said to Maxwell, "I think it's time you lost your virginity, for it's obvious you don't know what to do with a woman. I'm taking you to The Temple."'

'What does that mean?'

'The Temple is Dwight's brothel. He named it. It's just past the filling station. It has a black door and a bell, that's all. He took Maxwell there and put him in a room with the dirtiest hooker there. Then he charged him. When he took Maxwell back home he thrashed him. "Never bring the law to my door again," he said. "Just you remember I got another son, you better change if you want to stay around." It was the next day that Maxwell renamed himself Temple Jones. He told me that was how he wanted to be known, and he never mentioned it again.'

'He told me a man called Samuel Jones brought him up.'

'Samuel Jones was one of Dwight's customers. Maxwell named himself after a brothel and a trick.'

'It sounds like he didn't just pay one visit.'

'Oh no, he went through all the hookers.'

'Why was he born Maxwell Heed?'

'It's the name Dwight uses for business, Dwight Heed.'

'The police were hunting for Temple Jones, didn't you read about it in the papers?'

'Dwight's not real big on having papers in the apartment.'

'His picture was published; someone you knew would

have seen it.'

'If anyone did, they'd have been too frightened to come forward, too frightened of what Dwight would do to them.'

38.

'Holly said Dwight asked her to do things in bed,' I said.

'You want to know what Dwight does, Shepherd? He's real good in bed and slowly uses drink or drugs to get you to play roles he likes, and these roles make you feel real cheap.'

'What are they? Does he tie you up? How does he humiliate you?'

'He likes to watch women play with themselves. That's how it starts. Then he likes to watch women with other women. I could bring any woman back to the apartment that I want, just not a man. He ties you up, that was never a problem for me.'

'So you're saying he's a voyeur.'

'He participates too, but he likes to watch us do things first, dirty things.'

'And what are they?'

'You really want to know?'

'I don't. I want to find out if Temple Jones saw any of this.'

'Could be. What it boils down to is Dwight wants women to behave like whores.'

'Did he ride you?'

'Yeah, but there are far worse things he does.'

39.

She looked out of the window for a long time, and I thought
about leaving. The conversation felt soiled, and I didn't want
to probe her about what Dwight Fisher did to her in bed. But
I felt there was something missing, something I didn't know
about Dwight Fisher that would explain Temple Jones. It lay
behind Holly's silence, and I could see it in Francine's eyes.

'Temple Jones was riding my niece Marigold when
Holly stabbed him,' I said. 'He was using her bra as reins,
and I think he was going to kill her.'

'He learned it from Dwight. He used to watch his father
with women. Dwight would leave the door open. Once
Dwight had softened a woman up, he'd encourage her to
drink or take drugs, and then he'd start to get his kicks. I
think a lot of them were in blackout when he did it.'

'Did what?'

'He'd get them to act out porn. The riding was only part
of it.'

'Did he use bras?'

'No, he used a bridle. He saddled us up and screwed us
on the floor. He put it on real tight so we couldn't speak.'

'He treated you like animals. Why did you go along with
that?'

'I didn't remember he'd done it until I saw the film.
That's right, Shepherd, he films it and sells the films.'

'Holly refuses to talk about what he asked her to do.'

'Well, here are some of the things he likes. He'll ask you to masturbate, then in front of another woman. He'll tell you to do it to each other, then he'll screw you both. He'll talk dirty to you, tell you to say filthy things. He'll ride you, screw you, film you, then show you the film. He'll get you to use a strap-on jack with another woman. And he'll threaten to send the film to all your friends if you don't work for him.'

'You mean at his brothel?'

'That's right.'

'Is that what you've been doing? Working as a hooker?'

'Not any more, I'm his girl, he says, doesn't want me used. Shepherd, the things his clients are into are so foul, so sick, I don't even want to talk about them. The cops are the worst; they cuff you to hot radiators. They call you a whore as they fuck you with objects.'

'He made Temple Jones, that's where he learned it all. Dwight Fisher is responsible for the death of one of his daughters, the rape of his other one, the genital mutilation of my sister, and the violation of my wife.'

'And my son's dead.'

'You have to understand what he put us through.'

'I feel numb most of the time these days.'

'You know Marigold bore Temple Jones's child.'

'She had it after he raped her?'

'Holly forced her into it.'

'Dwight never talks about his daughters, only Felton.'

'Does Dwight know Temple Jones killed Felton?'

'No.'

40.

I had to get out of there. My head was swimming. I paid for the coffees and said good-bye to Francine, who was sitting at the table as I left. I walked to my pickup and drove out of the square. I noticed I was low on gas and stopped at a filling station. As I was paying I saw the young woman from the apartment. I could see she had a black eye. She began walking away, and I followed her to the next street. It was outside the brothel that I spoke to her. She looked scared and was fumbling in her purse, avoiding eye contact.

'Did he do that to you?' I said.

'I don't know what you said to him.'

'Is he still at the apartment? Is that where you've just come from?'

'He was a few minutes ago, but I wouldn't go there if I was you.'

'You don't have to let him treat you like this.'

'I don't have a choice.'

'He's got you working for him.'

'I'm his sexual prisoner.'

41.

She found the keys she was looking for and went inside. I stood there looking at the door after she closed it then walked back to my pickup, started it, and drove back to the apartment.

The door was open, and I walked into the hallway. As I reached the top of the stairs, I heard him call out from inside.

'That you? Come back for some more? Running out on me like that. You better come in here and strip, or it won't be my fist I'll use.'

I stepped inside, and he saw me. His face was a real mess.

He was standing in the living room. He was drunk, and he began to walk towards me.

'Get the fuck out of my apartment. Or I'm gonna kick the shit out of you,' he said.

'I'd like to see you try. You're lucky I didn't kill you.'

'You kill me, Shepherd, that's fucking comical. You caught me unawares earlier.'

'You turned Temple Jones against me.'

'Is that what you think?'

'You don't care for your daughters, probably because they're women.'

'Is that what you've come back to tell me?'

'But you also turned him against Felton.'

'Maybe I'll pay him a visit. How does it feel knowing Felton's my son?'

'You won't be paying him any visits, Felton's dead. Temple Jones killed him.'

'I think this is all bullshit. You're frightened I'll take your boy away from you.'

'He made it look like a hunting accident, it was in the papers if you don't believe me. He did it to get at you, Dwight.'

He looked at me with incomprehension, and I turned away from his degenerate face. I got in my pickup and drove out of New Hampshire, back to Vermont.

42.

All the way there I thought of the depravity in Dwight Fisher's face. He had declined so far morally since I knew him that despite the fact he'd kept his looks it was unpleasant to look at his face.

I had the answers I sought, and they explained Temple Jones, the offspring of a pimp who filled him with hatred and sexual depravity. There had been moments when I'd felt a sense of alienation in my own family, and it made sense to me now. I wondered if I'd sensed Felton was not my son.

But the revelation did nothing to lessen my grief for his loss. The paternal attachment I'd formed for him was too strong to be broken by the lies and actions of Temple Jones or Mary's deceit. And I thought about purity and realised that I was guilty too.

I loved Mary, and I wanted the past back. And so I returned to the red barn. I parked outside Holly's house and wondered if I was avoiding my house. I saw no lights on and walked to the barn in the twilight. As I stood outside it and thought of all the events that had happened there I realised the only way to recover from the violence Temple Jones had inflicted on us all was to root back into the past. For despite the fact that the barn reminded me of torture it also reminded me of pleasure and was a constant in the midst of violation.

I thought of the day I'd been rooting in the soil of my garden, when my fingers smelt of wild columbine and

sweetgrass, and I'd made love to Mary by the well. It was
the day I'd always believed, wrongly, Felton was conceived,
but the pleasure of the moment still remained in my memory.

I wanted the past back, in all its purity.

And so I drove home to Mary.

43.

She was in the kitchen making coffee, and she looked beautiful as she turned. She walked towards me and laid her hand on my arm.

Despite what lay between us, she was my wife and had been all these years. I sat down with her and told her what I'd found out in Lebanon. She listened as I recounted what I'd learned of Dwight Fisher and Temple Jones. When I finished I looked at her and the glow in her hazelnut hair, and I knew that my desire and love for her was greater than my need for bitterness.

Temple Jones had taken his revenge and been destroyed. There may never have been purity in any of us, but the belief in it was what mattered.

I thought of the letter Mary wrote to Dwight Fisher. And I looked at the picture of Felton on the dresser, my son.

I wanted to reclaim my past. I would not let Temple Jones take it away.

'Can you live with the deceit?' Mary said.

'You gave me a wonderful son,' I said.

I touched her then, I felt her hair and her face, then I kissed her on the mouth. I took her upstairs, and Mary undressed. I caressed and kissed her body. It was free of scars, and as I entered her on our marriage bed I thought that while there were internals scars in time they would fade. I would not let him steal my wife. I would not let his poison corrode the future.

Mary found her pleasure that evening, and I found mine, as we made love. And we ate dinner together, and I thought about Marigold and Holly.

44.

During the ensuing months Holly's mental state worsened. She stopped talking of the Bible, and I wondered if it had provided a thin veneer over what now emerged in her troubled mind. She became obsessed by filth, overdressing and avoiding eye contact with men she was convinced meant her and Marigold harm. And she began to believe that Joyce would return now that Temple Jones was gone.

With Holly's worsening mental state, Marigold was forced to look after Justin. She had no connection to the boy, whom she began to resent.

Mary and I tried to help. I feared the outcome of the situation. Justin was growing, and there were no provisions for his schooling. Holly had said she would tutor him at home but now showed no interest in the boy at all. We often found him on his own and unwashed when we went there.

I'd sit outside by the well as fall came on and think. The memory of making love to my wife there all those years ago and the belief I held that Felton was conceived there was filled with the invasive presence of Temple Jones now. I could hear the rowels of his spurs scraping the ground.

And I thought of how Dwight Fisher wanted what I had. Then I realised that the way to remove the thorns from my heart was to refuse to give it to him. My memories of my marriage and Felton before the revelations occurred were stronger than the hatred Temple Jones brought into our lives.

I looked about me and saw only the well and sunlight drifting through the golden leaves, and Mary's face beneath me, full of a fertile joy and infinite pleasure. To men like Dwight Fisher and Temple Jones the past is a place best avoided, but not to me. The past is my future. I live in a world of certainty.

EPILOGUE.

Over the years Justin's behaviour became harder and harder to discipline. Marigold had no job, and I tried to support her and Holly as best as I could. Justin began to display tendencies that troubled Marigold as he entered his teens.

One day she caught him looking at two girls as they changed in the dressing room of a store, and she punished him severely. She locked him in his room for days.

I felt she was seeing Temple Jones in him, watchful for his father's tendencies in the boy. But he seemed harmless to me, if unadapted to society.

On another occasion, Justin was brought home by the police. He'd been caught looking in a young woman's window while she was taking a shower. She wasn't going to press charges, but the police spent time talking to Marigold about the offence. When they left she was furious with him.

She hit him with a fire poker, caving in his skull. It wasn't until some hours later that she realised she'd killed him.

Holly called me and told me what had happened, and I drove there with Mary. When we got there we saw Marigold running to the barn. Holly was in the kitchen screaming. I left Mary with her and went after Marigold. I raced to the barn but stopped suddenly at what I saw. Justin was lying on the ground. He must have crawled out of the house and died. I was about to lean down and take his pulse when I heard a gunshot and I ran on.

I got there too late. Marigold had blown her head off with

the gun I'd bought for Holly.

I saw Holly and Mary running towards me. Then Holly started screaming again.

* * *

For many years after these events I thought of the past. My nieces were gone, and we were all altered by the man who had died but left behind a legacy.

I read that Dwight Fisher shot himself; he'd been arrested for rape. The article mentioned that his partner, Francine Rothwell, had left him and was working as a waitress.

Holly retreated into herself more and more after Marigold's suicide. Mary and I tried to help her, but her wounds were beyond that. And we tried to recover ourselves. Over time the memories faded and were replaced by the beauty of the countryside. And I felt that while Temple Jones had hid in the wilderness it was the thing that allowed his image to fade. And one year I felt the scars diminish. The colours of the leaves that fall were so magnificent I felt untroubled again.

Mary gradually began to forget what he'd put her through. But Holly's sense of loss and violation were something she never overcame. For although she began to talk more when we saw her she was profoundly altered. I became more concerned about her and offered for her to live with us, but she refused. Time finally allowed purity to return again. We were not hated. Vermont's beauty overcame the events that occurred in the barn.

One summer, years later, I made love to Mary by the well again, and when I kissed her she still tasted of mountain streams. And it was only us, and the one sound I heard was her voice as she whispered in my ear, 'It was only ever you, Shepherd.'

Use this link to sign up for advance notice
of Richard Godwin's Next Book:
http://wildbluepress.com/AdvanceNotice

Word-of-mouth is critical to an author's long-term success.
If you appreciated this book please leave a review on the
Amazon sales page:
http://wbp.bz/tpathreviews

More True Crime You'll Love
From WildBlue Press.

Learn more at: http://wbp.bz/tc

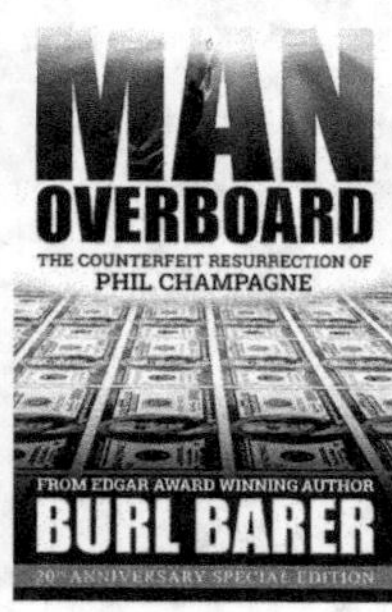

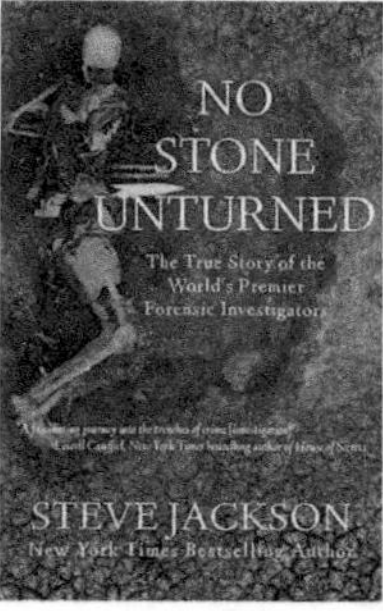

www.WildBluePress.com

**More Mysteries/Thrillers You'll Love
From WildBlue Press.**

Learn more at: http://wbp.bz/cf

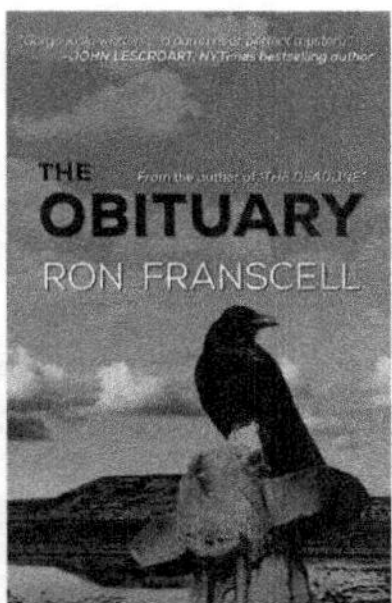

www.WildBluePress.com

Go to WildBluePress.com to sign up for our newsletter!

By subscribing to our newsletter you'll get *advance notice* of all new releases as well as notifications of all special offers. And you'll be registered for our monthly chance to win a **FREE collection of our eBooks and/or audio books** to some lucky fan who has posted an honest review of our one of our books/eBooks/audio books on Amazon, Itunes and GoodReads.

Let Someone Else Do The Reading.
Enjoy One Of Our Audiobooks

Learn more at: http://wbp.bz/audio

**Please feel free to check out more True CRIME books
by our friends at**

www.RJPARKERPUBLISHING.com